Fear and Journalism 2

Ben Patterson

Published by Cablue, 2025.

FEAR AND JOURNALISM 2

First edition. February 7, 2025.

Copyright © 2025 Ben Patterson.

ISBN: 979-8227081636

Written by Ben Patterson.

Table of Contents

Fear and Journalism 2

A Report by Roxie Vex, Galactic Truth-Seeker Extraordinaire

Chapter 1: Quick Draw

The range smelled like gun oil, scorched powder, and something faintly metallic that clung to the recycled air. A comforting blend. My boots scuffed against the rubber mat as I stepped up to my lane, rolling my shoulders before settling into a stance.

"You're hesitating," came a voice behind me. Smooth, controlled, and carrying the weight of quiet confidence.

I turned my head slightly, just enough to catch the range owner in my peripheral. He was a little older than me, maybe mid-thirties, with dark hair just long enough to tousle when he thought too hard about something. He didn't strike me as the thinking-too-hard type. He was the kind of man who did, acted, and let the results speak for themselves.

He moved in close, his body heat ghosting against my back. His left hand found my left shoulder, fingers pressing just firm enough to guide, not control. His right hand hovered over mine, close enough that I could feel the warmth radiating from his skin.

"You want speed, but your setup is working against you," he murmured, his breath barely skimming my ear. "Carrying lower might look good, but it slows you down. Too much weight pulling your hand down before the draw."

I exhaled through my nose, keeping my focus on the target ahead. "You saying I should hike it up to my hip like some over-eager academy grad?"

"Not saying you should. Just saying you'd be faster." His fingers flexed ever so slightly on my shoulder, subtle but suggestive. "Depends on what matters more—speed or style."

My hand hovered over my pistol, fingers itching for the draw. I knew my time was decent. Maybe not the best, but I wasn't competing with anyone. Not yet.

"Looks are half the game," I said, lips curving. "Nobody takes a geek seriously."

He huffed a laugh, low and amused. "Maybe. But I don't take dead people seriously either."

A challenge.

I tightened my stance, feeling the weight of the gun where it rested lower on my thigh. I knew the sensation, the rhythm. I could feel my body anticipating the draw before I even gave it the command.

"Alright, cowboy," I murmured, tilting my head just slightly toward him. "Show me."

I wasn't expecting his hand to actually move over mine. Wasn't expecting the shift in air as he leaned closer, pressing just a little more into my space. His fingers skimmed mine, barely touching, just enough to guide.

"Breathe in," he said softly.

I did.

"Breathe out."

My fingers tensed.

"Draw."

The gun was up and fired before I even registered the full movement, the shot cracking through the range like a statement. The hit landed clean on the target, not dead center, but close.

I smirked, tilting my head back to catch his expression. He was still close, close enough that I could read the flicker of approval in his dark eyes.

"Not bad," he murmured, his lips just barely curving. "Still think you need to adjust, though."

I cocked my hip, letting my gun settle back into place. "You gonna help me with that, or just keep breathing in my ear?"

His chuckle was deep, warm, and entirely too self-assured. "Why not both?"

This might just be my new favorite shooting range.

I huffed out a breath, rolling my shoulders. "Fine. Let's try it your way."

Jeff's mouth twitched at the corner, but he didn't say I told you so—he didn't have to. He was already reaching down, fingers brushing warm against my thigh holster as he unbuckled the strap. He slid the rig higher, adjusting the placement just below my hip bone. I didn't move, letting him work, feeling every brush of his knuckles as he refastened it snug against my waist.

His hand lingered. Just a second too long.

"Try it now," he said, his voice lower, smoother.

I flexed my fingers, letting my hand hover. It felt lighter, like it had been given permission to move freely. The weight of the gun wasn't dragging me down now—it was waiting, coiled, ready.

"Breathe in," Jeff murmured, back in my space, his left hand steady on my shoulder, his right ghosting just over mine.

I did.

"Breathe out."

I drew.

Fast. Faster than before. The gun was out and firing in one clean, fluid motion. The shot cracked through the air, and when I looked up, I couldn't help the slow grin pulling at my lips.

Dead center.

I holstered the gun, my fingers tingling from the draw. "Huh."

Jeff leaned in, his breath warm against the side of my face. "Told you."

I side-eyed him. "Don't get cocky."

His laugh was low, almost lazy. "I don't have to. You'll figure out I'm right soon enough."

We ran the drill a few more times, him close, always there, murmuring little adjustments, shifting my stance, his touch light but deliberate. Each shot was cleaner, more precise, the recoil snapping back into my arms like an old friend.

I was just settling into the rhythm when a familiar voice cut through the charged quiet.

5

"You two should get a room."

I didn't even have to turn around. That particular brand of deadpan sarcasm was unmistakable.

"Hey, Tuck," Jeff said, straightening but not stepping away.

I glanced over my shoulder. Tucker Quinn leaned against the partition, arms folded, his expression somewhere between amused and unimpressed. He was dressed like he always was—half rumpled, half like he'd wandered into the wrong decade, tie loose, sleeves pushed up, a coffee cup in one hand that was definitely not from this range.

"Didn't peg you for a shooting range guy," I said, sliding my gun back into its newly raised holster.

"I'm not," Tucker said, taking a sip of coffee. "But I was in the neighborhood and thought I'd see if you were still alive. Then I walk in, and what do I find? Roxie Vex, ace reporter, getting hands-on firearms training from our very own range Casanova."

Jeff smirked. "Jealous?"

Tucker made a face. "Deeply. Nothing gets me going like gunpowder and thinly veiled flirting."

I narrowed my eyes at Tucker as he stepped up to the booth next to mine, rolling his shoulders like he did this every day. He set his coffee cup down with deliberate care, then picked up one of the range pistols. His fingers curled around the grip with a kind of absent familiarity that I didn't like.

"Six shots," he said, flashing me that lazy, knowing smirk. "Last one to get 'em all off buys the other drinks at *The Cosmic Catastrophe*."

"You're on," I shot back.

I had him. No way Tucker Quinn—Mr. I-Won't-Carry-A-Gun—was going to beat me at this. I hovered my hand over my holster, ready to draw, ready to—

Brurrrt!

A quick, controlled burst, sharp and efficient.

I barely got my fingers around the grip before I heard the clunk of Tucker setting his pistol back down.

"You're kidding," I said flatly, turning to find him already hitting the recall button for his target.

The sheet zipped forward, stopping in front of him with six neatly grouped bullet holes, so tight you could slap a one-ounce silver round over them and not see daylight.

Jeff, completely unfazed, nodded at the target. "Nice spread."

Tucker smiled, the picture of smug satisfaction. "Vex, you owe me drinks."

I scowled. "You don't even carry a gun."

"I don't carry an elephant either," he quipped, picking up his coffee again, "but I know how to ride one."

Jeff chuckled and leaned against the divider. "He practices here all the time."

I turned back to Tucker, who was enjoying his damn coffee like he hadn't just hustled me. "You practice?"

He shrugged. "What, you think just because I don't carry, I don't know how to shoot? I like knowing I *could* if I had to."

I folded my arms, still eyeing his target like I could somehow argue with the results.

"Something wrong?" he asked, all innocence.

"Yeah," I muttered. "I was really looking forward to free drinks."

Tucker grinned. "That's the thing, Vex. They're still free. Just... not for you."

Jeff chuckled, but I just arched a brow. "That why you're here? To short circuit my love life?"

"Nope," Tucker said, then paused, considering. "Well, maybe. It's always entertaining. But actually, Dobbs is looking for you."

My smirk faded. "For what?"

Tucker tipped his head, all casual, but I caught the flicker of something underneath. Something that meant trouble.

"Said she's got a story for you," he said. "And you're gonna love it."

Chapter 2: The Trouble with Free Drinks

The Cosmic Catastrophe was going to cost me tonight. Not just in credits, but in dignity. Losing to Tucker Quinn in a shooting contest felt like losing a footrace to a guy who insisted on walking everywhere. But before I could dwell too much on that cosmic injustice, Tucker had to go and ruin my evening even further.

"Dobbs is looking for you," he said, like it was casual news, like Dobbs wasn't the kind of woman who could turn a perfectly good day into a twelve-hour descent into chaos.

I sighed, sliding my gun back into its freshly adjusted holster. "For what?"

Tucker took a sip of his coffee, because of course he wasn't in a hurry. "Said she's got a story for you."

A story. That could mean anything. Could be an exclusive, could be an excuse to chew me out for something I *allegedly* did.

I turned to Jeff. "Well, thanks for the hands-on training."

Jeff smirked. "Anytime, Vex."

He said it like he meant it, and I was absolutely going to overanalyze that later. But right now, I had a boss to see.

The *Galactic Gazette* newsroom was buzzing when I walked in, which meant one of two things—either something big had just broken, or the espresso machine was working again.

Dobbs' office was glass-walled, a fishbowl of authority, giving her a perfect view of the chaos she orchestrated. The blinds were half-drawn, which meant she was in that limbo between "not yet mad" and "about to be very mad." I figured I had a good ten seconds to brace myself before she saw me.

I stepped in, hands in my pockets, aiming for casual. "Chief."

Dobbs, a woman whose resting face could terrify war criminals, barely looked up. "Vex."

That was never a good sign. When Dobbs used my name without a *Roxie* in front of it, it meant she was in business mode.

She gestured to the chair across from her desk. I sat.

"You like free drinks, Vex?" she asked.

I narrowed my eyes. "Not when they come with a catch."

She smirked. "Good. Because this one's on me."

Now *that* was suspicious. Dobbs didn't buy people drinks unless she was feeling *really* grateful—or sending them into the kind of situation that required a last meal.

She slid a datapad across the desk. "You ever heard of Alton Yorrik?"

I frowned. "Sounds familiar. Related to Baron Yorrik?"

"His nephew. The smarter one. If that tells you anything."

It did. The Baron was a thug with money, a crime lord with a penchant for getting caught. If his nephew was the *smart* one, then that meant he was twice as dangerous.

I scanned the datapad. "What's he up to?"

"Novaterra-12."

I groaned. "Tell me this isn't another missing persons case."

She leaned back. "Okay, I won't tell you that."

I rubbed my temples. "Dobbs—"

"We're getting reports of people disappearing from the colony. Not just workers—whole families. They don't even bother packing up. They just *vanish*."

I frowned. "That's not Yorrik's usual game. The Baron was all about smuggling, not making people disappear."

Dobbs nodded. "Which is why we think Alton's running something different. Something bigger."

I tossed the datapad onto the desk. "And I'm supposed to go poke the hornet's nest?"

Dobbs smirked. "You're good at that."

She wasn't wrong.

I exhaled. "Alright. I'll check it out."

She nodded, satisfied. "And, Vex?"

I stood. "Yeah?"

She leaned forward just slightly. "Try not to get yourself frozen in carbonite or whatever it is they're doing to these people."

I grinned. "No promises."

As I walked out of her office, Tucker fell into step beside me, sipping his coffee like he didn't have a care in the galaxy.

"So," he said. "How dangerous is it?"

I glanced at him. "Why? You worried about me?"

He snorted. "No, I just want to know how much to bet on whether you make it back in one piece."

I smirked. "Buy me enough drinks tonight, and I'll make sure you regret that bet."

Tucker just grinned. "You're already making me regret it."

I made it to *Deadline* in record time, which was impressive, considering Tucker was still dogging my heels, throwing in helpful comments like, *"Maybe this time, don't get yourself nearly incinerated."*

"You say that like it was my fault," I shot back.

"You shot a guy holding a plasma grenade," he said, deadpan.

"He *was* holding it threateningly," I countered.

Tucker just shook his head and gave *Deadline* a once-over. "I still don't know how this thing is still flying."

"She likes me," I said, placing a hand on the hull. "Right, girl?"

The ship let out a soft hum, lights blinking to life as the cockpit hatch slid open.

"Roxie," came *Deadline's* familiar voice. "We both know I fly despite you, not because of you."

I grinned. "See? She loves me."

Tucker let out a long-suffering sigh. "Just don't get yourself killed."

I saluted him, then climbed into the cockpit. The seat molded around me like an old habit, and as the hatch sealed shut, *Deadline* ran her preflight checks.

"So, what trouble are we diving into this time?" she asked as I strapped in.

"Novaterra-12. People are disappearing."

Deadline made a thoughtful noise, a series of low hums and clicks as she processed. "Odds suggest either mass abduction, mass suicide, or a corporate cover-up. You tend to attract the first two."

"Gee, thanks." I flicked a few switches, feeling the ship vibrate under my fingertips. "Dobbs seems to think Alton Yorrik's behind it."

"The smart Yorrik?"

"That's what I said."

"Oh good. Maybe this time you'll actually get out without property damage."

I snorted. "Let's not get crazy."

The thrusters roared to life as *Deadline* lifted off, the station falling away beneath us. The asteroid belt sprawled out in the distance, chunks of rock floating like cosmic debris that had no idea how to mind its own business. We punched through the atmosphere and set a course.

"So," I mused, stretching my legs out. "What's the best-case scenario here?"

Deadline was quiet for a beat. "That this is all just an elaborate prank."

I arched a brow. "And the worst-case?"

"That you get taken, and I have to explain to Dobbs why she needs a new crime reporter."

I smirked. "Would you miss me?"

"I'd have to replace at least five internal systems that only function because you refuse to let me run them properly."

"So that's a yes."

Deadline huffed. "Just don't do anything stupid."

"Can't make promises I won't keep, babe."

I settled back as we rocketed into the black, Novaterra-12 waiting for us on the other side.

You got it! I'll keep it light, funny, and full of Roxie's usual charm. Let's dive into Chapter 3 and see where it takes us.

Chapter 3: Novaterra Nonsense

Novaterra-12 looked exactly like the kind of place where people went missing.

From orbit, the colony was an unremarkable blotch of prefab buildings squatting between jagged mountains and a dusty, too-red sky. There was nothing inviting about it—no lush greenery, no bustling spaceports. Just a bunch of structures that screamed *temporary*, even though they'd probably been here for decades.

Deadline cut the engines as we coasted into a docking bay. "Welcome to Novaterra-12. Please keep your hands and feet inside the vehicle until complete disappointment has been reached."

I popped the hatch and climbed out, boots hitting the metal platform with a satisfying clang. "At least act like you're impressed."

"Roxie, this place has the charm of a recycled air filter," Switch said as he stepped up t her side.

"You're just mad they don't have a high-end repair station."

"I'm mad they don't even have a *low*-end one."

Fair point. The docking area was depressingly empty, with only a couple of cargo crates and a single, underwhelmed port worker shuffling toward me. He looked about a hundred and ten, but that might've just been the lighting.

I flashed him my best *Hi, I'm a totally normal visitor and not here to stir up trouble* smile. "Hey there. Name's Roxie Vex, *Galactic Gazette*. Mind pointing me to whoever's in charge?"

He gave me a long, weathered stare, then shrugged. "That'd be Supervisor Krill. Admin office, second level."

"Great, thanks. And hey, I heard people have been going missing. That true?"

His eyes flickered toward the empty streets, then back to me. "You don't want to be asking about that."

"Oh, but I do."

He leaned in, lowering his voice. "Look, lady, I don't know what's happening, but one day people are here, and the next day, their quarters are cleaned out like they never existed. No warnings. No goodbyes."

"Sounds ominous."

He nodded sagely. "Also sounds like none of my business."

And with that, he shuffled away.

I sighed. "I *love* it when people are super helpful."

Deadline chimed in over my earpiece. *"I'm getting faint power fluctuations underground, but no official maps show tunnels or facilities beneath the colony."*

"So we've got mystery basement energy?"

"That's the technical term, yes."

I grinned. "Looks like we've got our first lead."

As Switch and I made our way toward the admin office, I passed boarded-up storefronts and flickering streetlights, all adding to the general *please leave before sunset* aesthetic. Whatever was going on here, the colony knew it—and they were terrified.

Krill's office was exactly what I expected: cluttered, stale-smelling, and about one strong gust away from total collapse. The man himself was a squat, sweaty bureaucrat with a comb-over that had lost its battle years ago. He barely looked up from his screen as I strolled in.

"Supervisor Krill?"

"Depends who's asking."

"Roxie Vex, *Galactic Gazette*. I'm here about the disappearances."

That got his attention. His fingers paused mid-keystroke, and he finally looked up, his expression immediately landing somewhere between *annoyed* and *existential dread*.

"There are no disappearances."

I arched a brow. "Oh, good. So you won't mind if I start asking around?"

"I *mind* very much."

"Cool. Thanks for your time." I turned to leave.

"Wait—"

"Sorry, can't hear you, already investigating."

As I strolled out, I tapped my earpiece. "Deadline, start scanning for underground entrances. Something tells me Krill isn't on the welcoming committee."

"You think?"

I smirked. "Call it a hunch."

With a mystery to unravel and the colony already giving me the cold shoulder, I had a feeling this job was going to be my favorite kind—dangerous, ridiculous, and probably requiring a good drink afterward.

Just another day in the life of Roxie Vex.

I looked at Switch. "You got a plan that *doesn't* involve blunt force?"

He studied the turret, then his optics flickered with something I *swore* was amusement. "Run really fast?"

"Absolutely not."

"Distract it while I throw you?"

I gaped at him. "Are you *trying* to get me killed?"

Switch shrugged. "Statistically, the odds are *only slightly* worse than your usual plans."

Before I could argue, he suddenly bolted out of cover, moving *faster* than anything that size had a right to. The turret whirred, tracking him—leaving me a wide-open shot at the power conduit behind it.

I grinned. *Clever bot.*

Raising my gun, I fired. The shot hit dead center, and the turret sparked violently before dropping limp.

Switch strolled back like he hadn't just *dodged bullets.* "There. Easy."

I holstered my gun and shook my head. "One of these days, that cockiness is gonna get you shot."

He smirked. "That's what you're here for."

I rolled my eyes and kept moving.

We weren't alone down here. Someone had built *something* under Novaterra-12, and whatever it was, it was worth hiding behind locked doors and automated weapons.

Which meant I was *definitely* in the right place.

With the turret now a useless heap of scrap, I moved forward, stepping over the still-smoking mess like I owned the place.

Switch fell into step beside me. "You do realize," he said, "that the security is only going to get worse the deeper we go?"

I smirked. "You *do* realize I have a history of ignoring really good advice?"

He sighed. "Noted."

Chapter 4: My Favorite Kind of No Trespassing Sign

If I had a credit for every time I walked into a place where I wasn't welcome, I'd have enough to buy a *second* ship just to store my bad decisions.

Novaterra-12 wasn't exactly rolling out the red carpet for me, but I wasn't expecting a warm welcome. I was, however, expecting to find an actual *clue* about what was happening here. So far, all I had was a sweaty bureaucrat, a colony full of people pretending not to be scared, and a hunch that the real action was happening somewhere *under* the ground.

Which meant I needed a way down.

"Alright, babe, tell me you found something," I murmured, tapping my earpiece as I strolled down one of the quieter streets. The buildings here were squat and industrial, the kind that looked like they were built in a hurry and would fall apart just as fast.

"Southwest quadrant," Deadline said. *"Behind what looks like a storage facility. I'm picking up some weird power fluctuations. Could be a hidden entrance."*

"Could also be a really bad generator."

"Yes, but that's less interesting."

"Fair point. Marking it now."

I rerouted, cutting through an alley that smelled like old metal and worse decisions. The storage facility wasn't much to look at—big, gray, and the architectural equivalent of *don't ask questions*. But around the back, just like Deadline said, there was something *off*.

For one, there were two very large, very serious-looking guys standing in front of a door that didn't match the rest of the structure. The building was dented and rust-stained, but this door was sleek, reinforced, and just *screamed* "I dare you to open me."

This was exactly my kind of problem.

I took a second to size up the guards. They had the standard *goon starter pack* look—black uniforms, military-style boots, and the subtle-yet-unmistakable posture of guys who got paid too much to frown and stand still.

"Deadline, what are the chances these guys are friendly?"

"Given that they have military-grade rifles and matching scowls? Low."

"Alright. Plan B."

"Do you even have a Plan A?"

"Yeah, Plan A was *ask nicely*."

I straightened my jacket and strolled toward the guards like I had every right to be there. Confidence was key. So was looking like someone annoying enough that they'd rather let me through than deal with me.

"Gentlemen!" I greeted, flashing a grin. "Is this the way to the *really* illegal stuff, or just the slightly illegal stuff? Because I have credits riding on it."

They did not smile.

Instead, the one on the left shifted just enough to subtly block the door. "This is a restricted area."

"Oh, *I know*. That's what makes it interesting." I leaned in conspiratorially. "Listen, I get it. Secret underground lair, probably something morally questionable going on—real hush-hush stuff. But between us? I *love* morally questionable things. So why don't we—"

The guy on the right reached for his rifle.

I sighed. "Okay, cool. Plan C it is."

Plan C was simple. Plan C was *run like hell*.

I bolted before they could react, sprinting toward the nearest stack of crates. Shots rang out, sparking against the metal as I slid behind cover.

"I take it they didn't let you in," Deadline said dryly.

"Oh, they were *so* close." I peeked out as one of the guards activated a comm unit. Not great. Reinforcements would be here soon, and I didn't have the time—or the firepower—to take on a small army.

Which meant I needed an exit. Fast.

Then I spotted it—a service hatch, half-hidden behind some crates. Small enough that they wouldn't be watching it, but just big enough for someone with questionable decision-making skills to squeeze through.

"Deadline, prep the engines. I might need a *very* fast ride out of here."

"That's always the assumption.'

I took one last deep breath, then sprinted for the hatch. More shots rang out. One of them clipped the edge of my jacket. That was going to be annoying.

I dove, yanking the hatch open and flinging myself inside.

It was dark. And cramped. And I was pretty sure something just scurried past my leg.

"Ugh. I *hate* Plan C."

The hatch slammed shut behind me, and I took a second to breathe. I was underground now, somewhere beneath the colony. Exactly where I wanted to be.

I just had to survive whatever came next.

As I crouched in the cramped darkness, I heard a metallic *thunk* behind me. I turned just in time to see Switch drop down through the hatch, landing in a perfect crouch like some kind of action hero.

"Where the hell have you been?" I hissed.

Switch straightened, adjusting the fit of his sleek combat plating. "Had to take a whiz."

I stared at him. "You're a robot."

He shrugged. "And yet, you bought it for a second."

I opened my mouth, then closed it.

"Don't think too hard about it," he added. "You'll hurt yourself."

I rolled my eyes. "Come on. We've got bad decisions to make."

He gestured toward the ominous underground tunnel ahead. "Ladies first."

With Switch now at my side—where he was *supposed* to be—we crept deeper into the tunnel. It was the kind of place where good ventilation went to die, filled with stale, metallic air and a suspicious dampness I didn't want to think too hard about.

The walls were old—*older* than the colony above. Rusted pipes ran along the ceiling, some hissing steam like they wanted to be in a horror movie. The lighting flickered just enough to be unsettling. Everything about this place screamed *bad idea,* which, naturally, meant I was going in further.

Switch's optics flickered as he scanned ahead. "You sure about this, Vex?"

"Oh, definitely not," I said, stepping over what looked like a suspiciously large rat. "But when has that ever stopped me?"

"You know, statistically, this kind of reckless behavior usually ends in—"

"—me finding a great story?" I interrupted.

"I was going to say *horrific injury,* but sure, let's go with that."

I ignored him and pressed on, moving deeper into the tunnel. We passed a series of old maintenance doors, most rusted shut, until we came to one that had been *recently* used. The panel was clean. The dust on the ground was disturbed. And, most tellingly, it had a keypad that looked way too advanced for an abandoned maintenance shaft.

I tapped my earpiece. "Deadline, tell me this thing is unlocked."

"I could tell you that, but I'd be lying."

I sighed. "Think you can crack it?"

"Given enough time, sure. But let me guess—you're not feeling patient?"

Switch stepped up, rolling his mechanical shoulders. "I got this."

Before I could ask what *this* was, he pulled back a fist and *punched* the keypad straight into the wall. Sparks flew. The panel shorted out. The door slid open with an almost *offended* hiss.

I stared. "Okay. That's one way to do it."

Switch dusted off his knuckles. "I *was* going to try hacking it, but this felt more... satisfying."

I smirked and stepped through the now-broken door. "Remind me to buy you a drink later."

The corridor beyond was different. Newer. Cleaner. It looked like someone had been maintaining it—a stark contrast to the rusty mess behind us.

"Someone's definitely been down here," I muttered.

Switch's optics flickered. "Yeah, and judging by the *fresh* security system, they're not looking for company."

That's when I heard it.

A low *whirrrr,* followed by the unmistakable sound of something *big* moving fast.

Switch grabbed my arm and yanked me back just as a turret dropped from the ceiling, spitting out a barrage of bullets that chewed through the floor where I'd just been standing.

I pressed against the wall, heart pounding. "Well. That's *rude.*"

Switch, completely unfazed, cocked his head at the turret. "Want me to punch that too?"

"Let's try *not* getting shot first."

I peeked around the corner, scanning the ceiling. The turret was tracking movement, its sleek black barrel shifting toward even the slightest twitch.

"Deadline, got any bright ideas?"

"You could try not getting shot."

"Wow. So helpful."

"Hey, you called me in the middle of my power nap. You want brilliance, give me a minute."

23

The hallway stretched on, leading us to another door—this one big, reinforced, and practically screaming *do not enter* in the way all truly interesting doors do. There wasn't a handle. No keypad. Just a single biometric scanner, the kind that required a palm print and probably belonged to someone important.

"Okay," I said, hands on my hips. "We either need an access code, a severed hand, or a miracle."

Switch flexed his fingers. "So, hand shopping?"

I gave him a look. "I was *joking.*"

"Yeah, so was I." He wasn't.

Before I could suggest *not* going full horror movie, my earpiece crackled.

"I got your miracle, babe."

I grinned. "Tell me you're about to do something impressive, Deadline."

"I do impressive things all the time, but you only notice when you need a door opened. Stand by."

A second later, the scanner beeped. The panel turned green. The door slid open.

I blinked. "I'm almost afraid to ask how you did that."

"Let's just say someone down here really needs to update their system security. Now hurry up. If I can hack it, someone else can too."

"Noted." I stepped through the now-open door, Switch right behind me.

We entered what looked like an underground operations center—dimly lit, lined with consoles and monitors, and eerily empty.

Which, frankly, was concerning.

"Where is everybody?" I muttered.

Switch scanned the room. "No recent activity. Whoever was running this place either cleared out or—"

The monitors flickered.

Switch went silent. I put a hand on my gun.

Then a voice crackled through the speakers—low, distorted, and entirely too amused.

"*Well, well. I was wondering when someone would finally come knocking.*"

I frowned. "I don't like that. I *really* don't like that."

The voice continued. "*You must be Roxie Vex. Reporter. Trouble-maker. Poor decision enthusiast.*"

I scowled. "Wow. Big fan, huh?"

"*Oh, absolutely. I love watching people dig their own graves.*"

Switch took a step closer. "Vex, this place is about to go bad."

"No kidding," I muttered.

The voice chuckled. "*I admire your persistence, Miss Vex. But you should have stayed on the surface. Now, you've left me with a very unfortunate decision.*"

Every screen in the room flashed red.

"*I can't let you leave.*"

Switch tensed. "Yep. *Called it.*"

Alarms blared. Doors slammed shut behind us. And just as I was about to start swearing, another sound filled the room—something heavy, mechanical, and very, *very* interested in making my life difficult.

Switch's optics brightened. "Now would be a good time for a Plan C."

I groaned. "Oh, for *hell's* sake—"

Then the wall behind the monitors *moved*.

And I suddenly had a *very* bad feeling about what was coming next.

Chapter 5: Big, Ugly, and Actively Trying to Kill Me

The wall didn't so much move as *disassemble itself* in a very expensive, very ominous way. Panels slid back. Pistons hissed. And out stepped what I could only describe as a war crime with legs—some kind of security droid, easily seven feet tall, armored like a tank and built like someone had looked at a demolition mech and thought, *Needs more murder.*

It had dual rotary cannons mounted on its arms, a head like an angry toaster, and a glowing red sensor that swept the room before locking onto *me.*

"Of course," I sighed. "Because *why not?*"

The voice from the speakers sounded far too pleased with itself.

"Meet the R-900. Designed for combat, crowd control, and unfortunately for you—pest extermination."

I put a hand on my gun, but Switch grabbed my arm. "Vex, that thing has more armor than sense. You are *not* gonna win a shootout."

"Then what's your plan? Sweet-talking it?"

"I was thinking *running,* actually."

The droid revved up its cannons. I decided running was *probably* a good idea.

Switch yanked me sideways just as bullets shredded the console where I'd been standing. Sparks flew. Alarms blared louder. We hit the ground and scrambled for cover behind an overturned desk as the R-900 continued its *very* enthusiastic attempt at turning us into modern art.

"You really should have stayed home, Miss Vex," the voice taunted.

"Yeah, well, I'm bad at good decisions!" I shouted back.

Switch peeked over the desk. "I'm gonna need about thirty seconds to work up a plan."

"Great, I'll just *distract* the killbot until then."

"Glad we're on the same page."

I rolled my eyes, took a deep breath, and did the only thing that made sense—I *popped out of cover and opened fire.*

The bullets hit. They also did absolutely *nothing.*

The R-900 turned its head slightly, like it was *offended* I even tried.

"Oh, *come on!*" I snapped.

It lifted an arm, cannons spinning up again.

Switch yanked me back behind cover right as the droid turned my position into scrap metal.

I gasped for air, heart pounding. "Okay, new plan—"

"Maybe don't get shot?" Deadline offered helpfully in my earpiece.

"Oh, *thanks,* genius! Why didn't I think of that?"

"You're welcome."

I shot a glare at Switch. "I hope that plan's coming *real fast.*"

He held up a small device—one of his energy pulse grenades. "I can overload its optics, but it'll only give us a few seconds."

"Fine. Do it."

"On three."

I nodded.

Switch counted down. "One... two..."

The R-900 stepped closer, raising an arm—

"*Three!*"

Switch lobbed the grenade over our cover. A second later, a *blinding* burst of blue light filled the room. The R-900 staggered, its sensor flickering wildly.

"GO!" Switch shouted.

I didn't need to be told twice.

We *bolted* for the exit. Switch hit the emergency override on the door. It screeched open, just wide enough for us to slip through.

We barely made it into the hallway before the droid recovered, turned, and—

BOOM.

The door slammed shut behind us.

I braced against the wall, breathing hard. "That... was *too close.*"

Switch straightened. "Yeah. Let's not do that again."

A heavy thud hit the door from the other side. Then another.

We exchanged a look.

I tapped my earpiece. *"Deadline. Tell me you've got an exit for us."*

"Working on it."

"Work faster!"

Switch looked down the corridor. "Where do you think this leads?"

I pushed off the wall and reloaded my gun. "Let's find out."

Because whoever was running this place had just tried to kill me.

Which meant I was *definitely* onto something.

Switch and I took off down the corridor, the sound of the R-900 pounding against the sealed door behind us. It wouldn't hold forever.

"Okay, okay," Deadline muttered in my earpiece, *"I found a potential exit. Good news—it's not far. Bad news—it's labeled 'Emergency Disposal Chute.'"*

I frowned. "That sounds suspiciously like a fancy way of saying 'garbage dump.'"

"Technically, it's a high-speed ejection tunnel designed for waste management."

Switch gave me a look. "So... garbage dump."

Deadline sighed. *"Yes, fine, it's a garbage dump. But it will get you out of there. Probably."*

I groaned. "Why is it *always* garbage chutes?"

A deep, metallic *boom* echoed behind us.

Switch glanced back. "I think the murder-bot is making progress on that door."

I gritted my teeth and kept moving. The hallway stretched ahead, dimly lit, pipes running along the ceiling, the air thick with the scent of oil and metal.

We rounded a corner—

And stopped dead.

Ahead of us, standing in front of the emergency disposal chute like a bouncer at a very exclusive nightclub, was another problem.

A *very* large problem.

A second security droid. Not as heavily armed as the R-900, but still way too much robot for my taste.

Switch exhaled. "They *really* don't want you leaving."

"Yeah, I got that."

The droid's optics flared to life, scanning us. Then, in a voice that somehow managed to be both monotone and aggressive, it spoke.

"Unauthorized personnel detected. Surrender or be neutralized."

I sighed. "They *always* say that."

Switch tilted his head. "I wonder what it would do if we actually surrendered."

The droid raised an arm. Its built-in plasma cannon started humming.

I deadpanned. "Oh, look. Death. What a shock."

The droid fired.

We dove in opposite directions as the blast scorched the floor where we'd been standing.

"I assume negotiations have failed," Deadline muttered in my ear.

I rolled behind a stack of crates. "Very insightful. Any other useful observations?"

"Yeah. You should really hurry up before the R-900 joins the party."

Switch had taken cover behind a wall panel. "Alright, Vex. Plan?"

I peeked out. The droid stood in place, tracking movement but not advancing.

"They must have programmed this one to guard the exit," I said. "It's not chasing us—it just wants us *dead*."

Switch considered that. "Then we need to make it *move*."

I grinned. "I like the way you think."

I unholstered my gun and fired off a few shots—not at the droid, but at a set of overhead pipes.

They burst, spewing high-pressure steam *right* into its optics.

It staggered back, momentarily blinded.

Switch wasted no time. He lunged, driving a metal fist into its torso. Sparks flew. The droid reeled but stayed upright.

I sprang forward, sliding across the floor beneath it, planting a magnetic charge on the back of its leg.

The moment I was clear, Switch hit the detonator.

BOOM.

The charge went off, and the droid toppled backward, slamming into the floor with a *crunch*.

I dusted myself off. "See? *That's* how you neutralize something."

Switch nudged the smoking wreck with his foot. "Yeah, yeah. Don't get cocky."

"Hate to interrupt your victory dance," Deadline cut in, *"but that door behind you? It's about ten seconds from being completely useless."*

We turned.

The reinforced door—the only thing keeping the R-900 from reducing us to spare parts—was buckling. Dents turned into cracks. A glowing red light shone through the seams.

"Oh, hell." I ran to the chute's control panel and hit the override.

The hatch hissed open, revealing a dark, narrow tunnel lined with grease and questionable fluids.

Switch eyed it. "I'm not gonna lie. That looks *terrible*."

I glanced back. The door behind us *exploded* inward, revealing the very, *very* angry R-900.

Before it could start ventilating us with high-speed projectiles, I shoved Switch aside, sending him sprawling behind a pile of debris. Then, without overthinking it (which, let's be real, is kind of my thing), I *dove* into the chute.

But instead of going full garbage-mode and plummeting to whatever horrors lay below, I snagged a side conduit, swung out, and dangled over the drop like some kind of spacefaring jungle gym enthusiast.

The R-900 stomped forward, cannons spinning up.

I grinned. "Aw, what's wrong? Big, scary war-bot afraid of a little slide?"

Its red optic flared. I had *maybe* a second before it turned me into a tragic cautionary tale about overconfidence.

And that's when Switch made his move.

He *launched* out from behind the wreckage like a robot-shaped missile, slamming full-force into the R-900's back.

For one glorious second, the war-bot teetered on the edge of the chute, servos whirring in confusion.

Then gravity got a say in the matter.

The R-900 *plunged* into the tunnel with all the grace of a vending machine being pushed off a cliff.

As it dropped past me, I managed a cheerful, "Buh-bye!" before it vanished into the darkness with a sound that could only be described as *a very expensive mistake.*

Switch leaned over the edge, watching it disappear. Then he turned to me, deadpan. "You were gonna let me get shot just to make a point, weren't you?"

I swung there, innocent as could be. "*Maybe.*"

He rolled his optics and reached down, grabbing my arm. With a not-so-gentle *heave,* he hauled me up and out of the trash tube.

I dusted myself off, grinning. "See? That went great!"

Switch crossed his arms. "We were almost *garbage.*"

"Yeah, but we *weren't*." I started walking. "Now c'mon. We've got a facility to snoop through, and no more homicidal security bots getting in our way."

He followed, muttering. "Next time, *you* get to be bait."

"Deal. As long as I still get to make fun of you afterward."

And with that, we ventured deeper into the facility, unimpeded, victorious, and *only slightly* covered in garbage juice.

Chapter 6: Not a Garbage Chute, But Somehow Still Worse

The good news? We weren't dead. The bad news? We were still inside this *very* illegal, *very* suspicious facility, and I was *incredibly* sure that if we didn't keep moving, someone was going to notice that their billion-credit kill-bot had just been yeeted into oblivion.

Switch and I crept down a narrow corridor, the lights overhead flickering with the kind of unreliable energy efficiency that screamed, *This place fails every safety inspection.*

"So," Switch said, "what's our next move?"

I gestured dramatically to the hallway ahead. "We explore, we gather intel, and we *absolutely* try not to find another murder robot."

Switch tilted his head. "Wouldn't mind finding another garbage chute, though."

I shot him a glare. "I *will* leave you here."

Before he could sass me back, a clunking sound echoed from up ahead.

We both froze.

Switch whispered, "Please tell me that was just the building settling."

A panel in the wall slid open.

Out stepped a human. A *regular, flesh-and-blood* human, wearing a lab coat, holding a datapad, and looking *way* too surprised to see us.

We all just... stared at each other.

The guy blinked. "Uh... you're not supposed to be here."

I smiled. "Neither are you."

"That doesn't even make sense."

Switch leaned toward me. "Solid comeback."

The scientist fumbled for something on his belt. Probably an alarm.

I grabbed his collar and yanked him close. "Hey, hey, easy, Dr. Suspicious. Let's not get the *whole* facility involved in this conversation."

He held up his hands. "Okay! Okay! No alarms! Just—who *are* you?"

I grinned. "Roxie Vex, *Galactic Gazette*. This is my associate, Switch. We're here because—" I gestured vaguely. "—*bad things* are happening, and I want to know about them."

His eyes darted side to side, nervous. "I—uh—I don't know anything."

Switch gestured to the datapad. "So if I look at that, it won't be full of information about said bad things?"

The guy clutched it to his chest. "It's *classified*."

I sighed. "See, *now* you've made me curious."

Before he could react, I swiped it right out of his hands.

He gasped. "Hey!"

I stepped back, scrolling through files. Switch loomed behind me, making sure our new friend didn't try anything *heroic*.

The more I read, the more my stomach tightened.

"Uh, Vex?" Switch asked. "Good news or bad news?"

"Oh, it's *always* bad news," I muttered.

Because this place? This wasn't just some illegal research facility.

It was a *human trafficking operation*.

And I'd just found the proof.

I scrolled through the datapad, my stomach twisting into a pretzel. This wasn't just a trafficking ring. It was worse. *Way* worse.

People weren't just being kidnapped. They were being *experimented on*.

Dissected. Augmented. Turned into *things* that weren't exactly human anymore. Some of the files had the word *"viable"* stamped across them. Others just said *"terminated."*

I felt the blood drain from my face. "Oh, this is *so* much worse than slavery."

Switch peered over my shoulder. "Wow. That's a sentence I wish I'd never hear you say."

I snapped the datapad shut and shoved it into his hands. "Send this to Deadline. Have it beam everything straight to the authorities."

"Already on it," Deadline chirped in my earpiece. *"And may I just say—yikes. This is some horror show level stuff."*

"Glad we're on the same page." I turned to our very anxious new friend, Dr. Suspicious. "Congratulations, Doc. You've just been promoted to *evidence.*"

His eyes went wide. "Wait—what? No, no, no, I can't leave! I'll be—"

I clamped a hand over his mouth. "Shhh. I hear what you're saying. You're worried, scared, probably thinking about how your life's work is about to be blown to hell. But here's the thing—you can either come with *us* and live, or stay here and see how your bosses feel about leaks."

Switch leaned in. "Spoiler: I don't think they'll send you a fruit basket."

The scientist made a muffled, panicked sound. I removed my hand.

"Fine!" he hissed. "Just—*don't let them kill me!*"

I grinned. "That's the spirit! Now let's get moving before—"

The alarm went off.

Red lights. Klaxons. A very loud, very automated voice shouting,

"Unauthorized personnel detected. Lockdown initiated."

I groaned. "Of *course.* I was *just* about to say something dumb like 'before anyone notices we're here.' Rookie mistake."

Switch grabbed the scientist by the collar. "We moving, or do you wanna keep standing here admiring your poor life choices?"

"Ugh, *fine,*" I muttered, drawing my gun. "But if anyone asks, I'd like it noted that for *once* I didn't cause the alarm."

We ran.

Heavily Armed Resistance: A Classic Exit Obstacle

We made it about twenty feet before the first wave of security burst into the corridor, weapons up.

I skidded to a stop. "Well. That was fast."

One of them barked, "Drop your weapon and surrender!"

I considered it for half a second. Then I shot out a ceiling panel above them, causing a whole mess of exposed wires and coolant fluid to rain down. They immediately started panicking, slipping, and swearing.

Switch whistled. "I *really* hope that wasn't important."

"Too late to care," I said, grabbing the scientist and pulling him toward the next hallway.

We sprinted through the facility, dodging guards, ducking under automatic turrets, and—at one point—using a rolling chair as an impromptu battering ram.

"Vex, not to rush you, but I'm picking up a lot of movement heading your way," Deadline piped in. *"Also, I'm parked in a restricted zone, and some very cranky people are asking me to move."*

"Tell them you're waiting for a friend," I panted, ducking behind a console as another burst of gunfire peppered the walls.

"I did. They're not buying it."

"Yeah, well, they're not gonna like how this ends either," I muttered, peeking around the corner.

More guards. Heavily armored. Heavily armed. Looking *real* serious about keeping us from leaving.

Switch crouched next to me. "Plan?"

I eyed the scientist. "Doc, you got any cool science-y tricks up your sleeve?"

"I'm a geneticist!" he squeaked. "I splice *DNA*! What do you want me to do, *threaten them with slightly improved lung capacity*?!"

I sighed. "Useless."

Switch pointed. "Vex, that panel over there—it's labeled 'Emergency Decontamination.'"

I grinned. "And *that* sounds like a thing we can exploit."

I pulled my gun and shot the control panel. The system *instantly* reacted, triggering high-powered sterilization mist and a whole lot of flashing warning signs.

The guards freaked. One of them shrieked, "OH GOD, IS IT A BIOHAZARD?!" and immediately bolted in the other direction.

"Yes!" I yelled after him. "Run for your lives!"

The rest hesitated—just long enough for me to grab the scientist and sprint through the mist, Switch covering our escape with a few well-placed shots at their feet.

The Unexpected Return of Our Favorite Murder Bot

We were just catching our breath when the **sidewall exploded.**

Not a door. Not a vent. The **wall.** Just *boom*, debris flying everywhere, and out stepped—

R-900.

It slowly turned its battered metal head toward us, **very** Terminator-like, but with slightly more *awkward politeness.*

"Hi there," it said cheerfully.

I stared. My gun was still raised, but my brain was trying to figure out if I was hallucinating or if this was real life.

Switch squinted. "Huh. Didn't we shove you down a chute?"

"Yes," R-900 confirmed. "That was **disorienting.**"

That's when I noticed the **giant dent in its head.** A big ol' caved-in section, like someone had taken a *space wrench* to it. Sparks fizzled from the damage, and its right eye flickered like a bad neon sign.

I had *zero* idea what that meant for us.

And then—

"Orders?" it asked politely.

Switch and I exchanged glances.

"*Orders?*" I echoed.

R-900 nodded, waiting patiently, like a dog that just got adopted by the people it was trying to maul five minutes ago.

I had **no idea** what was happening. Either the fall scrambled its programming, or we'd just unlocked a secret friendship mode. Either way, I wasn't about to waste this opportunity.

I cleared my throat. "Uh... clear a path to the hangar, please."

"Yes, ma'am," it said, **way too respectfully**, before turning and stomping off **to absolutely wreck security.**

Switch blinked. "Did you just **boss around** a murder bot?"

I shrugged. "I have a *very* commanding presence."

From up ahead, there was a lot of screaming, gunfire, and the unmistakable sound of someone getting yeeted across the room.

Switch listened, nodding. "You know... I could get used to this."

And with that, we followed *our new enforcer* to the exit.

The Final Stretch

By the time we reached the hangar, I was out of breath, out of patience, and *so* ready to get the hell off this floating nightmare.

"Vex, I see you," Deadline said. *"Ramp's down. Get your butts on board before things get real explode-y."*

"Music to my ears," I gasped, shoving the scientist forward. "Move it, Doc!"

We sprinted across the open tarmac, dodging gunfire from pissed-off guards who had finally gotten their act together.

Then a **big-ass mech suit** stomped into view.

I skidded to a stop. "Oh, *come on!*"

The mech's pilot, some smug-looking security goon, pointed a very large cannon at us. **"Stand down or be incinerated."**

Switch exhaled. "You know, I *do* enjoy variety in my threats."

"Right? Keeps it fresh."

The mech took a step forward, its weapon powering up.

And then—

Deadline's cannons fired.

The explosion *rocked* the hangar, sending the mech flipping *end over end* before it crashed *face-first* into a cargo container.

I blinked. "Did... did my ship just drop a *one-liner* before blowing something up?"

Switch nodded. "I think so."

I put a hand to my heart. "I have never been prouder."

We *bolted* up the ramp, the hatch sealing shut behind us.

"Alright, kiddos," Deadline chimed in, *"next stop, literally anywhere else."*

I collapsed into my seat, Switch dropping into his next to me.

The scientist just stood there, shaking, probably reconsidering *every* decision he'd ever made.

I pulled off my gloves, exhaling. "Well. That was a *productive* day."

Switch gave me a look. "We almost died."

I shrugged. "Yeah, but we *didn't*."

He sighed. "You are *so* bad at taking things seriously."

I grinned. "That's what makes me fun."

And with that, *Deadline* jumped to hyperspace, leaving that nightmare of a facility behind.

Chapter 7: Science Creeps and Federal Headaches

We dropped out of hyperspace, and for the first time in what felt like **forever**, I let myself relax. Switch and I had survived another suicide mission, Deadline hadn't been impounded, and best of all, we had one very terrified scientist to dump on **someone else's** lap.

That *someone* being **Gus Malloy.**

Gus was a fed, and in a galaxy full of bureaucratic deadweights, he was one of the *few* who actually gave a damn. He had helped me before—sometimes begrudgingly, sometimes enthusiastically, but always with a healthy mix of **sarcasm and caffeine dependency.** If I handed him a mess, he'd clean it up—*eventually*—but not without making me regret every life choice that led me to his office.

The scientist sat across from me, looking like a man who'd just been told he was about to meet the principal **and** the executioner at the same time.

Switch leaned toward me. "So, just to be clear, we're **not** spacing him, right?"

I sighed. "No, Switch. We're *not* spacing him."

Switch snapped his fingers. "Damn. Could've at least gotten enough credits for some better ship parts."

"Not how law enforcement works, buddy."

Switch grumbled. "Your rules are weird."

Deadline's voice chimed in. *"We're coming up on the Federal Outpost. Prepare to dock."*

I smirked. "Alright, time to ruin Gus's day."

Welcome to Gus Malloy's Office of Regret

The moment I stepped into Gus's office, he let out a **long, suffering sigh** and rubbed his face like he already knew I was bringing him a problem.

"Vex," he groaned. "Tell me you didn't just drop another **criminal** in my lap."

I beamed at him. "Gus, you wound me. This one's a **witness.**"

He eyed the scientist, unimpressed. "Uh-huh. And *why* does he look like someone just threatened to set him on fire?"

Switch raised a hand. "Because we *did.*"

The scientist gave a frantic nod. "They *absolutely* did!"

Gus pointed at me. "You can't just threaten people into testifying."

I shrugged. "I disagree."

He pinched the bridge of his nose. "Alright. What am I looking at?"

I handed him the datapad. "Science creeps turning civilians into *test subjects.*"

He scrolled through the files, his scowl **deepening** with every swipe.

"Son of a—" He stopped, exhaling hard. "This is bad."

"Uh-huh."

"Like, **intergalactic incident** bad."

"Yuuuup."

He dropped the datapad on his desk. "And you're **just now** bringing this to me?!"

"Well, in my defense, I had to **not die** first."

Gus groaned. "You are going to be the **death of me,** Vex."

I smirked. "Nah, I'll at least send flowers."

He muttered something I'm **pretty sure** was a death threat before turning to the scientist. "Alright, you. Start talking. Right now."

Switch clapped his hands. "And *that* is our cue to leave."

Gus pointed at me. "Vex, I *swear*, if you disappear before I have follow-up questions—"

I saluted. "Wouldn't dream of it."

I was **absolutely** going to disappear.

Because something told me **this mess wasn't over yet.**

Chapter 8: Second Stop—The Boss's Den

After dropping off Dr. Nightmare at Gus Malloy's House of Federal Headaches, I was more than ready to get back to the *Galactic Gazette*. There was something comforting about the smell of old coffee, overworked reporters, and the general air of impending deadlines that made me feel *at home*.

I set *Deadline* down smoothly at the Gazette's docking bay. Well, *mostly* smoothly. I only nicked one railing this time, which I considered a personal victory.

"I'd like to remind you that docking rails are not suggestions," Deadline grumbled.

"Noted," I said, not noting it at all.

As I climbed out of the cockpit, Switch popped out of his cubby, stretching like he had *actually* been cramped in there. "Next time, I call shotgun."

I patted his metal shoulder. "Not unless you plan on *shrinking* or I grow a second cockpit."

Switch grumbled something about unfair accommodations but followed me inside anyway.

Inside the Lioness's Den

Dobbs's office was as welcoming as ever, which is to say **it wasn't.**

She was sitting behind her desk, looking like she hadn't slept in a week, which probably meant the paper had just broken another huge story. Either that, or she had been stuck reviewing **expense reports.**

Dobbs barely glanced up as I strolled in. "Vex."

"Boss."

She pointed at a chair. "Sit. Talk."

I flopped into the chair, tossing my datapad on her desk. "Wrapped up another nightmare. *Super* fun. Human experimentation, a dash of mad science, and *oh yeah*, an entire hidden lab full of goons with bad aim."

She picked up the datapad and scrolled through the files, her expression **not changing one bit.** "Uh-huh. And the authorities?"

"Gus has it."

Her brow arched. "And he hasn't killed you yet?"

"Not for lack of trying."

Dobbs snorted, setting the datapad aside. "Good work, Vex. I'll have our people get this prepped for publication. You did get quotes, right?"

I blinked. "Uh."

She sighed. "You forgot to get quotes, didn't you?"

"...Maybe."

Dobbs pinched the bridge of her nose. "One of these days, I swear..." She took a deep breath. "Fine. I'll have someone pull the legal statements from the feds. In the meantime, get some rest. You look like you got tossed down a garbage chute."

"I *did* get tossed down a garbage chute."

She blinked. "I wasn't being literal."

"Lucky guess."

Before Dobbs could respond, the door swung open, and in **sauntered Tucker Quinn,** looking far too smug for someone who wasn't armed in a galaxy full of people who liked shooting at me.

"Well, if it isn't Roxie Vex, back from another reckless escapade." He leaned against the doorframe. "You keep this up, and I'll have to start a betting pool on your life expectancy."

I gave him my sweetest, most insincere smile. "Tuck, always a pleasure. What are you doing here? Get lost on the way to covering another *intergalactic clown war?*"

He smirked. "Nope. Just here to remind you that while you're out dodging blaster fire, I'm *winning* awards."

"Participation trophies don't count."

Dobbs cut in before we could escalate. "Quinn, get out."

He held up his hands, grinning. "Fine, fine. Just wanted to say *hi*." He gave me a wink before strolling out.

I rolled my eyes. "He gets *way* too much enjoyment out of being insufferable."

Dobbs smirked. "You say that like you don't."

I gasped. "Boss. I am a *delight*."

She didn't even dignify that with a response. Instead, she pulled up a new file on her screen. "Alright, since I know rest isn't in your vocabulary, here's your next assignment. Something weird is brewing on a colony called...

I hurried away before she could finish.

Paying Debts and Ignoring the Unusual

Tucker had barely made it five steps down the hall when I caught up to him, stepping into his path with a casual lean against the elevator panel. He gave me a smirk, clearly expecting some sort of snarky farewell.

I smiled sweetly. "I owe you drinks."

His smirk deepened. "You actually admit it?"

I crossed my arms. "I honor my debts. Even when I lose under *questionable* circumstances."

"Questionable? I recall the bet being *six shots, first to finish wins*. You just didn't specify semi-auto vs. burst fire."

I scowled. "It was implied!"

"Not my problem if you can't read between the bullets, Vex."

The elevator doors slid open. I gestured inside. "Come on, hotshot. Let's go cash in before I change my mind and spend my credits on something useful—like bribing bartenders to water down your drinks."

Tucker chuckled and stepped in. "The Cosmic Catastrophe, then?"

"Obviously. Where else can you get a halfway decent drink and a guaranteed brawl?"

The Cosmic Catastrophe – Where Normalcy Comes to Die

The Cosmic Catastrophe was its usual mess of dim lights, questionable odors, and the underlying hum of a bar just waiting for something to explode.

Tucker and I took a booth near the back, mostly because it had the least amount of *mystery stains* on it. I flagged down the bartender, a four-armed Andralax named Spiv, and ordered whatever swill passed for whiskey that night.

Spiv didn't even ask if I wanted it neat. He knew me too well.

Tucker swirled his glass, studying the amber liquid. "So, what's next for you? Another dive into the galaxy's underbelly?"

I took a sip. "Likely. Dobbs handed me a new case, but I haven't looked yet. I figured I'd at least *pretend* to take a break before getting shot at again."

He raised his glass. "To pretending."

I clinked mine against his. "To pretending."

We drank.

And that's when the weirdness started.

It was subtle at first. The music skipped, like someone had nudged a record player—except we were in a digital age, and there was *no reason* for that to happen.

Then, at the bar, a man took a sip of his drink and immediately *turned invisible*. His clothes were still visible—floating in midair—but the man himself? Gone.

Tucker didn't even look up from his drink. "That guy just turned invisible."

I took another sip. "Yep."

The guy's friend nudged the floating clothes. "You okay, buddy?"

"Yeah, I think so," the invisible man said. "Feels kinda tingly."

His friend sighed and waved at Spiv. "Hey, I *told* you to stop mixing the house whiskey with dimensional rifts!"

Spiv groaned, already reaching for some sort of counteragent. "It was *one* drop! He's just phasing a little—he'll be fine in a few minutes."

48

Tucker and I exchanged a glance but didn't comment. This was just *Tuesday* at the Cosmic Catastrophe.

Then a chair in the corner started floating. Not like someone had lifted it—like it had *decided* to no longer obey gravity. It twirled lazily in the air before flipping upside down and hovering there, completely at peace with its newfound existence.

Tucker finally arched a brow. "Okay, I'll bite—how do you think *that* happened?"

I shrugged. "Either someone's had one too many drinks, or the laws of physics took the night off."

We watched as a drunk guy tried to sit on the floating chair, only for it to *flip away* the moment he got close. He frowned, muttered something about *stubborn furniture*, and stumbled off to find another seat.

The bartender set a new drink in front of the invisible guy, who was slowly *phasing back into existence* like a bad hologram.

Tucker knocked back the rest of his whiskey. "You ever wonder if we've just *gotten used to this kind of thing*?"

I swirled my own glass. "Tuck, if you haven't figured out by now that *we are the weirdest thing in the room*, you haven't been paying attention."

He smirked. "Fair point."

We finished our drinks, paid up (because I am nothing if not honorable), and stepped out into the night, leaving the floating chairs and flickering men to their business.

Just another evening at the Cosmic Catastrophe.

Chapter 9: High Heels, Higher Stakes

I have a simple rule about rich people—if they aren't trying to rob you blind, they're trying to sleep with you. Sometimes both, in that order.

Tonight, I got to test that theory firsthand.

Dobbs had sent me to cover what she referred to as *an easy gig*—just a bit of white-collar crime, some financial fraud, maybe a little corporate embezzlement. Nothing too dramatic, just a few rich folks shifting numbers around like a shell game while pretending to be *pillars of galactic society*.

The job? Show up at the charity gala thrown by infamous corporate overlord Marcus Langstrom, schmooze my way through the upper crust, and figure out which billionaire was up to no good.

For this, I needed to dress the part.

Dressed to Kill (Figuratively... For Now)

I slipped into a gown so sleek it felt illegal. Black, backless, with a slit so high it was practically tax-exempt. My hair was up, my makeup was perfect, and my heels were tall enough to qualify as weapons.

Switch stood by, giving me a once-over with his glowing optics. "I feel like I should be charging people just to look at you."

I smirked, adjusting the diamond bracelet I'd borrowed from *someone who didn't know it was missing yet.* "Let's hope the billionaires feel the same way. Try to look menacing, will you?"

"I'm a seven-foot combat droid in a suit." He straightened his tie. "I *define* menacing."

With that, we headed into the gala, ready to rub elbows with people who thought taxes were *optional suggestions.*

Welcome to the Shark Tank

The Langstrom estate was exactly what you'd expect—gold-trimmed everything, chandeliers the size of small moons, and a guest list made up of people who owned planets but had probably never *set foot* on them.

The moment I walked in, all conversation within a ten-foot radius *halted*.

Billionaires were *not* used to being speechless. These were men who could buy entire city blocks just to *shut up* someone they didn't like. And yet, there they were, gripping their glasses of imported Jupiter gin like their *souls had left their bodies*.

I gave them my best *oh, am I distracting you?* smile and strolled into the room.

"Play nice," Switch murmured.

"Always."

The First Victim: Winston Armitage III

Armitage owned half the asteroid mining operations in the Vega Belt and had the kind of money that could fund *actual* time travel. He approached me with the confidence of a man who had never been told *no* in his life.

"You must be new to these events," he said, turning on what I assumed was *his* version of charm.

I sipped my champagne. "Oh? What gave me away?"

He gestured vaguely. "You stand out."

I tilted my head. "Is that a compliment or an accusation?"

His smile wobbled. "Both?"

This was too easy.

"So, Mr. Armitage," I purred. "How's business? Any *recent financial audits* giving you trouble?"

He actually *choked* on his drink. "Why would you ask that?"

I leaned in, giving him just enough of a view to make him forget his own name. "Oh, just making conversation. But I hear the tax boys have been sniffing around some *interesting transactions* lately..."

He made an excuse so bad it was practically a confession and vanished into the crowd.

Switch chuckled through our comms. *"One down. Who's next?"*

The Second Victim: Desmond Vale

Vale was a shipping magnate who had turned *smuggling* into an *art form.* His favorite pastime was pretending he was legitimate.

He sidled up to me, all smooth confidence. "I don't believe we've met."

I gave him my most dazzling smile. "We haven't. But you look *very* familiar."

"Do I?"

"Yes... oh!" I gasped, pretending to have just placed him. "You were in the news! Something about—what was it—*undocumented cargo*?"

Vale went *stiff.* "Ah. A misunderstanding."

"Of course," I said sweetly. "So tell me, how do you *accidentally* move two hundred tons of contraband across Federation lines?"

Switch, standing stoically behind me, let out the softest chuckle. Vale made a noise that sounded like *panic in human form* and bolted.

"Two down," Switch noted.

"Too easy," I muttered.

The Real Target: Marcus Langstrom

Langstrom, the host of the evening, had been *far too calm* all night. That meant he was hiding *something big.*

I let him find me.

"Miss Vex," he said, taking my hand and kissing it like we were in some kind of holo-drama. "You are *a vision.*"

I gave him a slow smile. "Flattery's nice, Mr. Langstrom, but I'm more interested in *figures* than compliments."

"Ah," he chuckled, sipping his drink. "A woman who enjoys numbers. And what figures interest you tonight?"

"Oh, you know. Offshore accounts. *Missing* assets. Funds that *vanish* before auditors can see them."

His smile *barely* faltered.

"Interesting topics for a charity event," he said smoothly.

I shrugged. "I like to keep things exciting."

Langstrom *knew* I was onto him. And that's when the real game began.

The Escape and the Aftermath

By the end of the night, I had gathered enough intel to ensure *at least* three billionaires wouldn't be sleeping easy. Switch and I slipped out before security *conveniently* escorted us off the premises.

As we strolled down the grand marble steps, Switch glanced at me. "You *enjoyed* that."

"Obviously." I grinned, adjusting my wrap. "When else do I get to dress like this and ruin the lives of the one-percent?"

Switch nodded. "Fair point."

Behind us, we heard one of Langstrom's goons say into his comm, "She was *too* hot. That was the problem. Nobody could focus."

I smirked. *Damn right.*

"Let's get out of here before they realize what just happened," I said.

Switch gestured toward *Deadline*, waiting for us in stealth mode. "After you, Miss Vex."

And with that, we left *yet another* party in ruins.

Chapter 10: Space Chase and Shenanigans

I don't usually let anyone ride shotgun in *Deadline*'s cockpit. Partially because I like my personal space, but mostly because the ship wasn't initially built for two.

Still, as we prepped for takeoff, I gestured for Switch to join me up front. "C'mon, big guy. You earned it."

Switch hesitated. "Technically, I always ride in the ship—"

"Yeah, yeah, but this time, you get to *sit* up here instead of curling up in your cubby like some kind of murder-dog. Consider it an honor."

He slid into the second seat behind me, his large frame making the cockpit feel about as roomy as a broom closet. I toggled the launch sequence, and *Deadline* smoothly lifted off, burning atmosphere as we left the planet behind.

That's when the fun started.

Uninvited Company

I had just leaned back, ready to bask in a rare, *uneventful* getaway, when *Deadline* chimed.

"Incoming vessel, unidentified, vector locked on our six," she reported.

Switch glanced at the scanner. "That's a little close for comfort."

I sighed. "Of course, some moron thinks tailing me is a good idea."

The ship in question was small, fast, and armed just enough to be *annoying*. I gave it a few minutes, hoping it would wise up and veer off.

It didn't.

"Alright, buddy," I said, flipping some switches. "You wanna play? Let's dance."

Dogfight Delight

I yanked *Deadline* into a sharp barrel roll, snapping around to face the unknown ship head-on. The sudden move must've surprised them, because they hesitated just long enough for me to *introduce myself*—by way of a warning shot across their nose.

"Back off," I hailed them. "Or I turn your cockpit into a convertible."

Their response?

A volley of laser fire that *barely* missed my wing.

"Oh, *hell yes*," I grinned. "Now it's fun."

Switch sighed. "Why do you *enjoy* this?"

"Because I'm *good* at it," I said, throwing *Deadline* into an inverted dive to dodge their next shots. "And because adrenaline is cheaper than therapy."

We danced through space, dodging and weaving, throwing shots back and forth. The pilot was decent—quick reflexes, solid maneuvers. But I was *better*.

I let them think they had the upper hand, dragging them into a chase pattern before slamming my thrusters and *suddenly* cutting speed. They shot past me, right into my targeting lock.

"*Gotcha.*"

One well-placed hit to their engines, and their ship sputtered like a drunk trying to start a fight he *already lost*.

The Interrogation—Roxie-Style

With their ship dead in the water, I latched on with a tow cable and hailed them again.

"Alright, genius. Who sent you?"

No answer.

Switch flipped a few external comm settings, amplifying my voice *directly* into their cockpit.

"HELLO?!" I bellowed. "YOU'RE NOT MAKING ME REPEAT MYSELF, ARE YOU?!"

A strangled yelp came through. "O-okay! It was Langstrom! He paid me to make sure you *didn't* make it off-planet!"

I smirked. "See? That wasn't so hard. Now, sit tight while I *personally* drag your sorry ship to the feds."

I turned to Switch. "Set a course for the precinct. Let's go press some charges."

"You mean *dump a bounty hunter's broken ship in their parking lot*?"

"Exactly."

Switch leaned back. "I *love* our job."

With our prisoner in tow, we made our way to the precinct—because nothing says *justice* like publicly humiliating a guy who thought he could take me down.

Dragging a beaten, half-functional bounty hunter's ship to a federal precinct is the spacefaring equivalent of strutting into a courtroom with a smoking gun, a signed confession, and a big, stupid grin.

I wasn't just proud of myself—I was *thrilled*.

Switch must've noticed, because as we settled into our approach vector, he said, "You're in an unusually good mood."

I shot him a sideways smirk. "What can I say? Some people do yoga. Some people meditate. *I* blow holes in things that try to kill me. It's called self-care."

Switch nodded sagely. "Shooting something *is* your version of a spa day."

"Exactly."

"Do I need to be concerned?"

I patted him on the shoulder. "Only if you ever try to kill me. You'd never do that, would you, buddy?"

He didn't answer right away.

I squinted at him. "Switch."

"Just thinking," he said finally. "I don't believe so. I mean, *currently*, no."

"Good enough," I muttered. "Now, let's go rub this in some faces."

Delivering the Package

We touched down at the fed precinct, our unwanted guest still neatly tethered to *Deadline* like a particularly ugly hood ornament. As soon as we powered down, I popped the canopy and hopped out, cracking my knuckles like I was about to walk into a boxing ring.

Switch followed, rolling his shoulders. "So, what's the plan?"

"Plan?" I said, grinning. "I'm going to walk in there like I own the place, make Malloy *deeply regret* not giving me a badge, and enjoy myself."

"Of course," Switch muttered.

The precinct doors hissed open, and I strolled in like I was fashionably late to an awards ceremony. Agents and officers bustled around, busy with actual crimes that didn't involve my personal vendetta. I spotted Gus Malloy near the back, frowning at a data pad like it had personally insulted his mother.

Perfect.

Pressing Charges, Roxie-Style

"Guuuuus!" I called out, voice high and sing-songy.

The precinct collectively sighed. I have that effect on law enforcement.

Malloy didn't even look up. "Vex."

I slapped the data pad with everything I had uncovered about the hit job down onto his desk. "Good news! I brought you a case, a suspect, and an *excellent* reason to buy me a drink."

He finally looked up, his tired eyes flicking between me, the data pad, and the monitor showing *Deadline*'s external cams—where my captured ship still hung like a sad, beaten puppy.

"You tow this in yourself?" he asked, rubbing his temples.

"With love and care," I confirmed. "And I'd like to press *so* many charges."

Malloy sighed, picked up the pad, and scrolled. "Langstrom sent someone after you?"

"Bingo." I leaned against the desk, trying to look like a responsible citizen. "That ship outside? Piloted by the idiot who admitted to it. *On tape*, might I add. And I figure, since I *technically* saved the day again, you should consider my whole *unlicensed vigilante* thing more of a *community service* situation."

Malloy pinched the bridge of his nose. "Roxie, you know the law doesn't—"

"Do I look like I care?" I grinned. "Because I *don't*."

Switch folded his arms. "She really doesn't."

Malloy exhaled slowly, then tapped a few things on his terminal, no doubt filing paperwork he *absolutely* didn't want to deal with today.

I clasped my hands together. "Oh, and when you haul Langstrom in for questioning, make sure to tell him *I* sent you. Really let it sink in that I keep ruining his day."

Malloy leaned back in his chair, eyes full of regret. "I *should've* arrested you a long time ago."

"You say the sweetest things."

Victory Lap at the Booking Desk

I made my way to the booking desk, where a couple of feds were dragging in my bounty hunter buddy. He looked even sadder up close—like someone who realized he should've stayed home today.

I leaned against the desk as they started processing him. "Hey, pal. Quick question—how's it feel to be *the worst* bounty hunter I've ever met?"

He glared. "I had you!"

"Sure you did," I cooed. "Right up until you *didn't*."

The officer booking him smirked. "She got you good, huh?"

The bounty hunter slumped. "I hate this job."

I patted his shoulder. "Next time, try your luck hunting someone *less* awesome."

He muttered something unkind under his breath. I *chose* to ignore it, because I was in a *great* mood.

I turned to Switch. "Alright, let's go before I start buying these guys coffee out of pity."

Switch, who had been watching the whole thing with a mix of amusement and mild horror, just nodded. "You got what you wanted?"

"Oh, *absolutely*," I beamed. "Now, let's go spend Langstrom's bounty money on something *stupid*."

As we left the precinct, Switch shook his head. "You *really* needed to shoot something today, didn't you?"

I grinned. "So much."

Chapter 11: Just Another Day at the Office

Strutting down the spaceport tarmac, heels clicking against the deck, Roxie Vex was on top of the world. Adrenaline still coursed through her veins, her pulse drumming a rhythm that matched the triumphant grin stretched across her face. Her latest bounty hunter problem was now Malloy's headache, and she'd taken down his sleek, overpowered ship with style.

"I mean, did you see that last move, Switch?" she asked, twirling once for emphasis, the hem of her shimmering dress catching the artificial light. "Barrel roll into a reverse thrust? Textbook genius. Textbook. That guy thought he had me dead to rights, but nope—outmaneuvered, outgunned, and now he's enjoying the fine hospitality of Galactic Enforcement. You may begin praising me now."

Switch, towering beside her, kept pace with his usual unhurried gait. "I will require more time to process the overwhelming magnitude of your piloting brilliance," he deadpanned.

Roxie huffed. "Oh, come on. I was incredible."

"I did not say otherwise."

"And yet, no applause."

Switch inclined his head as if considering. "Shall I offer a slow clap? Or would you prefer a pre-recorded standing ovation?"

She swatted at his metallic arm. "You are so lucky I like you."

The ramp to Deadline lowered as they approached, and the ship's voice—dry as ever—chimed in. "Welcome back, Oh Grand Vanquisher of the Inept. Shall I preemptively warn the Gazette staff that you're arriving in full peacock mode?"

Roxie smirked. "Damn right, you should. And log my kill, Deadline. That bounty hunter's ship was fast—not as fast as me, but

61

still. Might as well get credit in case some other moron thinks they can cash in on me."

"Logged," Deadline confirmed. "Though I should note that a prudent individual would consider lowering their profile. You, however, are Roxie Vex."

Roxie's grin widened. "Exactly."

By the time they reached the Galactic Gazette, she still hadn't stopped talking about the dogfight. She sauntered into the bullpen like she owned the place—which, in a way, she did. At least, she had the biggest headlines and the most property damage claims.

The moment she stepped through the doors, the newsroom erupted.

A chorus of whistles, catcalls, and "whoo-hoos" filled the air as reporters turned from their screens, throwing out compliments ranging from the sincere to the wildly inappropriate.

"Damn, Vex! You get a new side gig?"

"Somebody warn high society—she's dangerous and well-dressed!"

"Switch, what do you charge to be a personal bodyguard?"

"Tucker! Tucker, get in here—Vex is gorgeous!"

Roxie took it all in stride, tossing her hair over her shoulder and striking a dramatic pose. "Yes, yes, I know—I'm a vision. Hold your applause. Actually, don't."

From across the bullpen, Tucker Quinn poked his head out of his office, took one look at her, and gave a slow, appreciative nod. "Rox, I gotta say, if you ever want to ditch investigative reporting and become a full-time heartbreaker, you've got my vote."

"Noted," she said, then leaned on the nearest desk. "Now, who wants to hear about the time I outflew a bounty hunter with a top-tier ship and zero morals?"

Dobbs' voice cut through the chaos. "You could've been killed, Vex!"

Roxie turned, flashing her boss the most innocent smile she could muster. "But I wasn't. And I got the story." She held up her datapad.

Dobbs sighed, rubbing her temples. "Of course, you did." She snatched the pad from Roxie's hand and pointed a warning finger. "One day, your luck is going to run out."

Roxie winked. "Then I'll just make more."

Switch let out a mechanical sigh. Deadline, still patched into the newsroom's speakers, muttered. "For the record, I tried to warn her."

And with that, Roxie Vex kicked back in a chair, still radiant, still invincible—at least for today.

Chapter 12: The Fine Art of Not Giving a Damn

There are two versions of me. One—the one in the black flight suit, guns strapped to my hips, striding through crime dens like I own the place—scares the hell out of most people. The other—the one in an evening dress, hair pinned up just so—makes high society forget how dangerous I am. Truth be told, I didn't know which version I liked better.

But right now, I was neither. Right now, I was off duty.

Tucker and I ducked into our favorite dive, *The Cosmic Catastrophe,* a place so disreputable that it hadn't even bothered to put a name on the door. That was probably for the best, considering how many times it had been raided, shot up, or otherwise legally frowned upon. Yet, somehow, the drinks were always cold, the booths always intact, and the clientele just the right mix of dangerous and too drunk to care.

We ordered our usual—whiskey, neat, for me; some ridiculous fruity concoction for Tucker, complete with a tiny umbrella. He swore up and down it was an ironic choice, but I wasn't convinced.

The place was as lively as ever. A couple of reptilian traders were loudly arguing over what I could only assume was a smuggling deal gone wrong. A four-armed card shark flipped a deck of plasma-etched playing chips between his fingers like a magician. And in the corner, a ghostly, translucent figure sat hunched over a drink, which was impressive considering it had no visible mouth.

"Dead man drinking," I muttered, nodding toward the ghost.

Tucker glanced over, unimpressed. "Yeah, well, last time I was here, he was winning at darts."

I slid into a booth in the back, Tucker following with his ridiculous drink in hand. "You ever gonna order something that doesn't look like it came from a vacation brochure?"

He smirked. "What's the point of a dive bar if not to make ironic drink choices?"

I rolled my eyes and took a sip of my whiskey. "You pacifists are a weird breed."

Tucker just laughed. "Pacifist, sure. Weird? Definitely. But I like to think I'm focused. You chase the big, bad, and bullet-riddled. I chase the absurd."

"And that's crazy," I said.

"Only to you."

It was an old argument. He didn't carry a weapon. He didn't believe in violence. And yet, somehow, he made it through this ridiculous galaxy in one piece, armed with nothing but a sharp wit and a recorder.

Me? I wasn't wired that way.

"Just saying," I continued, swirling my glass, "one day, one of these stories of yours is gonna get you into trouble you can't talk your way out of."

"And that's what I have you for," he said, raising his glass with a grin.

I clinked mine against his. "Damn right."

Behind us, a chair spontaneously caught fire. No one reacted.

I took another sip. "Hey, you remember that time we watched that guy get stabbed, but he turned out to be a hologram, so the real guy was just standing there laughing?"

Tucker nodded. "Yeah. Good night, that one."

A lizard-like patron slid across the bar, screaming. No one helped.

"Or the time the jukebox started playing music from a planet that exploded a century ago?" I mused.

"That one was spooky," Tucker admitted. "But still, probably just an old signal bouncing around."

The bartender, a grizzled old alien with six eyes, calmly tossed a bucket of water on the flaming chair. A new patron took the seat immediately. Business as usual.

I leaned back, stretching. "You know, sometimes I wonder if we should drink somewhere less cursed."

Tucker grinned. "Where's the fun in that?"

I had to admit—he had a point.

Chapter 13 Friends in Low Places

Pirate territory. The phrase alone was enough to send most respectable people running in the opposite direction. Me? I packed an extra gun.

Dobbs' latest assignment had me deep in the heart of lawless space, on a planet so thoroughly owned by criminals that the only law enforcement presence was the occasional bounty hunter scraping up the leftovers. The cops had tried to hold it once—tried and failed spectacularly. My job was to find out how that happened.

So, naturally, I went straight to the source.

The head of this little pirate paradise called himself Rogan Kane. No flashy title, no over-the-top moniker like "Bloodfang" or "Captain Death." Just Rogan Kane. And when I met him, I understood why—he didn't need theatrics.

Kane was a tall, broad-shouldered man with salt-and-pepper hair and a face that looked like it had seen plenty of action but never lost its composure. He wore a crisp, dark suit—not a single bloodstain, which was impressive given his line of work—and carried himself with the easy confidence of a man who didn't just control this planet, but was this planet.

"Miss Vex," he greeted smoothly as I stepped into his office—a surprisingly refined setup with leather chairs, expensive liquor, and a view of the bustling city below. "I must say, I've been looking forward to this meeting."

I arched a brow. "You a fan of the Gazette, or just curious if I'd be dumb enough to show up?"

His lips quirked. "A little of both."

Switch, ever the killjoy, stepped up beside me, towering over the room like a seven-foot chaperone. "If this is an ambush, I'd advise against it."

Kane chuckled, completely unfazed. "No ambush. I prefer conversations over firefights. More productive." He gestured to the chair across from his desk. "Please, sit."

I hesitated just long enough to make it clear that I was the one making the decisions here—then I sat. Kane poured two glasses of amber liquid and slid one my way. Switch made a small noise of disapproval, which I ignored.

"So," I said, swirling the drink but not sipping yet, "the cops came in swinging, and you sent them running. How?"

Kane leaned back, utterly relaxed. "It's simple, really. You surround yourself with competent people and put them where they'll do the most good."

I snorted. "That sounds suspiciously like management advice, not organized crime strategy."

He smiled. "You'd be surprised how much overlap there is."

I had to admit, he had a point. The difference between a crime syndicate and a corporation was mostly a matter of PR. One had stockholders, the other had hired guns.

"And the police?" I pressed.

Kane shrugged. "They thought brute force would win the day. We had better force, better strategy. They relied on bureaucracy. We relied on results."

There was something unnervingly reasonable about him. No ranting about power, no threats, no pretense that he was anything but what he was—a man who made things work.

"Smart," I admitted. "And now you've got yourself a nice little haven for criminals."

He inclined his head. "I prefer to think of it as an autonomous zone."

I laughed. "You really should've gone into politics."

"Maybe in another life."

The conversation shifted after that, drifting into more neutral territory. Kane asked about my work, my travels, my opinions on the state of the galaxy. He was charming, polite, and utterly aware that I was probably the biggest threat to his operation he'd ever meet. And yet, he didn't seem to mind.

By the time I left, I'd made a decision—Kane was worth keeping as an informant. He wanted to take out his competition. I wanted stories. It was practically a symbiotic relationship.

Switch, of course, had other thoughts.

"This is a terrible idea," he said the moment we were alone.

"Oh, relax, Switch," I said, waving him off. "He likes me."

"That is precisely the problem."

I smirked. "Come on, where's your sense of adventure?"

"Currently filing a report on your reckless disregard for self-preservation."

I rolled my eyes. "It's called networking, big guy."

Switch let out a mechanical sigh. "One day, your version of 'networking' is going to get us both shot."

I patted his arm as we boarded Deadline. "And when that day comes, you can say 'I told you so.'"

Switch muttered something about inevitable doom, but I was too busy thinking about the exclusive I'd just landed.

Pirates, politicians, cops—it was all the same game. And I always played to win.

Chapter 14: Two Sides of the Same Dirty Coin

Criminals kill for personal gain. Doesn't matter if it's selling stolen star frogs, knocking over a bank, or lighting up a whole block in a turf war—at the end of the day, somebody wants something, and they don't care who they have to step on to get it.

And on the other side of that same dirty coin? Government overreach. The galaxy's biggest gang, dressed in uniforms and fancy titles, using laws and loopholes instead of blasters to take whatever they want. Power grabbing more power. A whole machine built to keep itself running, no matter how many people it grinds down in the process.

And caught in the middle of it all?

Just folks.

People who don't give a damn about crime or law, just about getting through the day. The ones who just want to work, eat, drink, and sleep without someone kicking in their door or raising their taxes or "reallocating" their water supply to some high-rise they'll never afford to live in. Live and let live—that's all they wanted. And more often than not, they were the ones who got stepped on first.

I sat at my desk in the Gazette bullpen, feet kicked up, staring at my ceiling tiles like they held some kind of universal truth. My last few cases rolled through my head like a bad holovid montage.

Slave traders. Chains. Shock collars. Cargo bays full of people who weren't supposed to be cargo. I still saw their faces when I closed my eyes.

Human experimentation. Labs hidden behind corporate front doors, all clean and clinical—until you saw the subjects. The ones who'd survived, anyway.

Some real nightmare fuel.

And then there was Kane.

Didn't seem like that kind of guy. Hell, compared to the monsters I'd taken down recently, he was practically a model citizen. He didn't deal in flesh. Didn't run any creepy, back-alley science projects. Just carved out his own little piece of the galaxy, beat the cops at their own game, and kept his people in line.

And sure, the key word there was his—but was that any different from the way a corporate exec owned a planet's workforce? Or the way some bureaucrat on a cushy salary decided who got food shipments and who got ration bars?

Maybe Kane was just another brand of power player, another cog in the big, corrupt machine. But maybe—just maybe—he was onto something.

And maybe it was worth another trip to his no-go zone.

Not to see him, necessarily.

But the people living under his so-called protection.

I could talk to the locals, the shopkeepers, the workers, the ones just trying to survive. See if they felt safe. See if they felt like they were living or just existing under another man's boot.

Because if Kane really was just another power-hungry thug, I'd find the cracks.

And if he wasn't?

Well. That would be a hell of a story.

Chapter 15: Crime, But Make It Functional

If you'd told me a month ago that I'd be flying into pirate-controlled space to do positive coverage on a known criminal, I'd have laughed in your face and then probably stolen your drink for the crime of saying something that stupid near me.

Yet, here I was.

I touched down on Bannon's Rest, a dusty little rock just inside Kane's so-called "autonomous zone." Nothing flashy, nothing too lawless—at least not on the surface. Just a place where people had been knocked around so many times that they finally stood up and said, Alright, everyone get the hell out. We'll handle it from here.

I walked through the marketplace, expecting the usual signs of a criminal stronghold—shady deals in alleyways, twitchy people watching their backs, maybe a pickpocket or two dumb enough to try me.

Instead, I found normal.

Not just normal—functional.

A woman selling fresh fruit off a hovercart waved at me. A group of kids ran past, playing some game that involved a lot of shouting and zero respect for personal space. A few guys sat outside a repair shop, drinking and arguing over the best kind of engine coolant like their lives depended on it.

I stopped at a stall selling fried... something. "So," I asked the guy behind the grill, "what's it like living under Kane's rule?"

The cook—big guy, missing two fingers, excellent mustache—gave me a look like I'd asked him if water was wet. "Kane? He's alright."

"Alright?" I repeated. "You do know he's a criminal, right?"

The guy snorted and flipped whatever mystery meat was sizzling on his grill. "Lady, I've lived through three gang wars, two corporate takeovers, and one planetary governor who taxed us so hard we had to start trading in cans of soup because nobody had money left. You know what all those people had in common?"

I leaned on the counter. "Enlighten me."

"They didn't give two wits about us." He jabbed his spatula in my direction. "Kane? He's different. He got rid of the people using us as cannon fodder and told the rest of us to run things how we saw fit. You don't start trouble, nobody bothers you. You work, you eat. You break the peace, you're the problem."

That sounded an awful lot like... I don't know... basic civilization.

A woman at the next stall, stringing up some handmade jewelry, chimed in. "Kane ain't from here. He just got sick of the killing, same as the rest of us. So when things got bad, he helped us boot out the idiots in charge—both the criminals and the so-called 'lawmen'—and set up a system that actually works."

"You trust him?" I asked.

The cook shrugged. "Trust? No. I don't trust anyone with power. But I trust that he wants things to stay stable. And that's more than I can say for the last dozen people who tried to run this place."

It was weird. I'd interviewed people about crime bosses before. Usually, I got a lot of quiet, nervous glances. A few half-hearted "He's a good guy"s from people who had blasters pointed at them off-camera. But this?

This wasn't fear.

This was respect.

And that made me uneasy.

Because Kane had every hallmark of a criminal mastermind. He ran an empire. He had absolute control over his territory. He had resources, people, power. By every traditional definition, he was an outlaw, a kingpin, a man who should've been on every wanted list from here to the galactic core.

So I had to ask—who exactly defined Kane as a criminal?

The people here? They didn't see him that way.

The government? They'd failed these people so hard they had to be forcibly removed.

The cops? They lost the fight and ran home with their tails tucked.

So was Kane the bad guy? Or just the guy who won?

There was only one way to find out.

I'd have to do what I did best.

Dig.

Chapter 16: The Sweet Taste of Crime (or Maybe Just Sugar Kane)

Dobbs read my article three times.

Once in silence.

Once with an exasperated sigh.

And once with the kind of face that suggested she was mentally composing my obituary.

Finally, she leaned back in her chair, ran a hand down her face, and said, "I should've given this assignment to Quinn."

"Excuse me?" I put a hand to my chest, all fake offense. "Dobbs, I am insulted. I bled for this story."

"You bled?"

"Metaphorically."

She squinted at me. "That usually means no."

"Well, I could have bled. Switch is always telling me I'm one bad decision away from a hospital bed."

Dobbs exhaled sharply through her nose. "You're one bad decision away from a casket, Vex."

I waved that off. "That's just life, chief."

She pinched the bridge of her nose, probably mentally weighing the pros and cons of early retirement. "You were supposed to cover crime, Roxie. Real crime."

"This was crime!" I protested. "Kane's technically a criminal."

"Is he?" Dobbs shot back. "Because according to your article, he's running a well-organized, crime-free utopia where the biggest problem is whether or not Sugar Kane is an embarrassing nickname."

"Okay, but—"

"—and instead of doing hard-hitting investigative journalism about actual illegal activities, you wrote me a piece on how wonderful it is to live in a place with no property taxes."

I leaned forward. "Right?! It is wonderful! Did you know that—"

"I don't care," she said flatly.

I sat back. "Cold."

Dobbs tapped the article on her desk. "This is Quinn's beat, Vex. The weird beat. You? You cover crime. Actual crime. You know—murder, smuggling, blackmail, political corruption. Not whatever this is."

"So... not even a little impressed with my deep dive into economic reform?"

She rubbed her temples. "Get out of my office."

"On it." I grabbed my hat—okay, I don't wear a hat, but it felt like a hat-worthy moment—and strolled out before she could throw something at me.

Later that night, I was at *The Cosmic Catastrophe* with Tucker Quinn, drowning my editorial sorrows in a drink that may or may not have contained actual fuel-grade alcohol.

Quinn, in his usual easygoing way, leaned back in the booth and smirked at me. "So, let me get this straight. You went looking for crime, and instead, you found the world's nicest criminal?"

"Pretty much."

"And Dobbs is mad because instead of exposing some great scandal, you basically wrote a tourism brochure for Kane's territory?"

"That is an oversimplification," I said, taking a sip. "But yes."

He chuckled. "Rookie mistake, Vex."

I frowned. "I am not a rookie."

"No, but you forgot the golden rule: never write an article that makes the editors question why you wrote it and not me."

"I did wonder why you weren't assigned this."

He grinned. "Because real crime is your beat, and I cover the absurdities of the universe. And you, my dear, have apparently stumbled into my world."

I mulled that over. "I guess it was kinda weird."

"Kinda?" He raised an eyebrow. "The big bad crime boss runs a utopia with no government interference, no crime, and a single land tax payment? That's weird, Roxie."

I opened my mouth to argue. Closed it. Sipped my drink.

"...Okay, yeah. That's weird."

Quinn spread his arms. "Welcome to my world."

Before I could respond, the guy at the bar erupted into flames.

I barely even blinked. Quinn didn't look up from his drink.

The bartender, completely unfazed, grabbed a fire extinguisher from under the counter, doused the guy in foam, and went right back to drying glasses.

The guy—still smoldering—grumbled, shook off the foam, and sat back down like spontaneous combustion was just a mild inconvenience.

Neither Quinn nor I acknowledged it beyond him sighing and muttering, "Third time this week."

Across the room, an argument between a three-eyed lizard man and a sentient cloud of gas ended when the gas made a very impolite noise, and the lizard man huffed out in a rage.

"Must've been something he said," I quipped.

Quinn snorted.

At another booth, a woman with a cybernetic arm was arm-wrestling a guy whose entire body was cybernetic. The woman was winning.

I sipped my drink again. "So, the real question is... did I like this one?"

Quinn tilted his head. "Did you?"

I thought about it.

All things considered... I did. It had been weird, sure. And not my usual kind of story. But it was interesting. It was different. It was fun.

And, if I was being honest with myself, it had been nice to write something that didn't involve dead bodies and explosions for once.

I smirked. "Yeah. I think I did."

Quinn clinked his glass against mine. "Then congratulations. You've officially crossed into the realm of the absurd."

I grinned. "Guess I have."

The guy at the bar caught fire again.

Neither of us moved.

The bartender sighed, grabbed the extinguisher, and went through the whole process again.

As the guy sputtered through a mouthful of fire suppressant, I leaned back, taking it all in.

Maybe I had just stepped into Quinn's world.

Maybe I liked it.

Chapter 17: A Course Correction (Sort Of)

Kane's office was as tidy as the man himself—clean, organized, and suspiciously lacking in obvious crime. No piles of stolen credits. No shady goons with menacing glares. No helpless victims tied to chairs. Just Kane, leaning back in his chair, reading the Galactic Gazette like he was some upstanding citizen keeping up with the news.

As Switch and I stepped in, Kane didn't even glance up. He just flicked a finger toward the chairs across from his desk.

We sat. Well, I sat. Switch loomed.

Kane turned a page, still absorbed in whatever thrilling piece of journalism had caught his attention. I had a sneaking suspicion it was my article.

Finally, he folded the paper, set it down, and looked at me.

"So," he said, "you get it?"

Did I?

I thought I did. I thought I understood that Kane wasn't running a crime syndicate so much as a better government than the actual government. Which, yeah, was weird. But my beat was crime. And Dobbs was breathing down my neck because, apparently, tax reform didn't count as high-stakes investigative journalism.

I leaned forward. "My editor's pissed at me."

Kane smirked. "I'd be shocked if she wasn't."

"She thinks I went soft. That I lost the thread. I need crime, Kane. Real, solid crime. Can you help me out?"

That smirk of his grew a little sharper. "Crime, huh?"

"Yes. You know—smuggling, heists, blackmail, something illegal." I gestured around. "I mean, you are a criminal, right?"

Kane chuckled. "That depends on who you ask."

I rolled my eyes. "Okay, fine. Can you at least point me in the direction of some actual criminals?"

He folded his hands on the desk. "Tell me, Vex—what do you know about Dorianus' moon?"

I frowned. "Pirate stronghold. Kind of a lawless dump. Full of smugglers and thieves."

"Bingo." He leaned back. "They deal in stolen goods—some legal, some not so much. Find out where the pirates snatched the contraband, and you've got yourself a story."

Now that sounded more like it.

I grinned. "Now we're talking."

Kane picked up his newspaper again. "Happy to help."

I stood up. "Thanks."

"Good luck," he said, flipping a page.

Switch and I turned to go. But just as I reached the door, Kane called out—

"Oh, and Vex?"

I looked back.

He grinned. "Try not to get yourself killed."

"No promises."

And with that, I was off to find myself a real story.

Chapter 18: Pirate Shopping Spree

The problem with pirate strongholds isn't that they're dangerous—I mean, they are, but that's kind of a given. The real problem is that they smell terrible.

Dorianus' moon was no exception. The entire place reeked of engine grease, unwashed bodies, and that special kind of "mystery meat" smell you get when something's been on a grill too long and might have started as either a rat or a rival smuggler.

"Alright," I said, stepping off Deadline's ramp and into the mess of a marketplace. "Let's find some stolen goods."

Switch, standing at my side like the world's most intimidating chaperone, responded dryly, "Yes, let's definitely announce that loudly and publicly."

"Relax," I said, tossing him a grin. "These are pirates. They love selling stolen goods. It's their whole thing."

The market was a chaotic mess of stalls and makeshift storefronts selling everything from high-end weaponry to questionably sourced antiques. If you needed a black-market kidney or an ex-government droid with the serial numbers scraped off, this was the place.

I stopped at a vendor selling what looked like rare alien artifacts. I picked up a fancy gold statuette of some multi-armed deity. "This legit?"

The vendor, a lizard-like guy with three eyes and a suspiciously toothy grin, spread his arms. "Of course! Ancient relic, very rare! Found in deep space ruins!"

Switch leaned in, scanning it. "This was manufactured six months ago."

The vendor hissed. "I said deep space ruins."

I set the statue down. "Pass."

We moved on, weaving through the crowd. Everywhere I looked, someone was peddling something shady. Weapons, jewelry, crates stamped with shipping labels from companies that definitely hadn't meant to deliver here.

I stopped at another stall, eyeing a stack of luxury handbags. "Huh. I was expecting more... illicit goods."

The vendor, a short, grumpy-looking woman, snorted. "Lady, you think crime lords' girlfriends don't want nice things? A lot of these are stolen straight from high-end spaceports." She picked up a sleek red purse. "This one? Came off a senator's wife last week."

I whistled. "Nice work."

She grinned. "You want it?"

I considered it. "I do like red..."

Switch crossed his arms. "You are not buying stolen goods."

I sighed. "Fine. But know that you just ruined a perfectly good fashion opportunity."

We continued on, until I spotted something truly interesting—a group of pirates unloading a crate marked with the insignia of a major corporate supplier.

Bingo.

I sauntered up, all casual. "Hey, boys, what's in the box?"

One of the pirates, a big guy with an eyepatch (because of course he had an eyepatch), eyed me. "None of your business."

I flashed him a charming smile. "Oh, but it is my business. See, I'm a journalist, and I love a good smuggling operation. Where'd you get the goods?"

The pirate groaned. "Not another reporter."

"Not just another reporter," I corrected. "The reporter."

The guy rolled his eye. "Look, lady, we don't exactly keep receipts."

Switch loomed behind me, his glowing optics narrowing. "Perhaps you should start."

Eyepatch grumbled. "Look, we don't steal everything. Some of it we buy off the back of other smugglers' ships. Some of it falls off transport freighters. And some of it comes from... let's call them questionable corporate arrangements."

I crossed my arms. "Meaning?"

Another pirate chimed in, a wiry guy with a cybernetic arm. "Meaning sometimes we steal it, and sometimes corporations pay us to 'lose' shipments so they can claim insurance money."

I raised an eyebrow. "Interesting."

Eyepatch sighed. "That was interesting. And now you're going to leave."

I grinned. "Oh, I am leaving. But not before I write a scathing exposé on how corporate bigwigs are in bed with smugglers."

The pirates groaned in unison.

Switch placed a firm hand on my shoulder. "Perhaps it's time we go before we get shot."

"Fine, fine." I backed away, still smirking. "Pleasure doing business, gentlemen."

As we walked back toward Deadline, I clapped my hands together. "Dobbs wanted a real crime story? Oh, she's getting a crime story."

Switch muttered, "And probably a hit squad to go with it."

I waved that off. "Details."

I had a scoop, I had a lead, and I had a moon full of pirates who now really wished I hadn't shown up.

Good day's work.

Chapter 19: How to Make Enemies and Influence Smugglers

You ever get the feeling you've kicked a hornet's nest, and the hornets are just waiting to sting you in the face?

That's where I was.

I had my story—corporate execs and smugglers working together to pull insurance fraud on a galactic scale. It was juicy, scandalous, and guaranteed to make some very powerful people extremely unhappy. Which, for me, was just another Tuesday.

Switch and I had barely made it back to Deadline before I got the first sign that maybe—maybe—I had poked the bear a little too hard.

My ship's console was flashing with an incoming message from Dobbs. That was already unusual. Dobbs wasn't a call you in person kind of boss unless someone was suing, shooting, or threatening to light the office on fire.

I accepted the transmission, and Dobbs' face flickered onto the screen, looking about as pleased as a cat stuck in a bathtub.

"Vex."

I saluted. "Chief."

"You have got to stop pissing off people with private armies."

I frowned. "Which ones this time?"

She sighed, pinching the bridge of her nose. "Roxie, the corporations you just dug up dirt on? They're big. They have lawyers. And more importantly, they have mercenaries."

I waved that off. "Yeah, yeah. Big scary men with guns. You've sent me after worse."

She ignored that. "I just got a friendly little note from a very expensive legal firm telling me that if we run your story, we'll be dealing with more lawsuits than a malfunctioning airlock company."

I grinned. "That means it's a good story."

Dobbs scowled. "It means you've officially made yourself a target. Again."

I scoffed. "Dobbs, I'm always a target."

"That's not a good thing, Vex!"

Before I could retort with something about job security, Switch—who had been scanning comms this whole time—interrupted. "Roxie."

His voice had that just a heads-up, we're probably about to be murdered tone.

I turned to him. "What?"

He turned one of Deadline's external cameras on-screen.

"Oh," I said.

Because sitting outside, just on the edge of sensor range, were three unmarked ships that screamed hired muscle.

Dobbs, still on the call, noticed my silence. "What is it?"

I pointed at the screen. "You know how you said I made myself a target? Turns out, you were right."

She groaned. "Of course I was right. What are you gonna do?"

I cracked my knuckles. "Well, first, I'm going to see if they actually try anything."

"And then?"

I grinned. "Then I'll give them a very educational lesson in why it's a bad idea to mess with a woman whose ship is basically a flying arsenal."

Dobbs stared at me for a long moment, then just muttered, "Why do I even bother?" before ending the call.

I turned to Switch. "Alright, big guy. Ready to give these goons something to think about?"

Switch's optics glowed just a little brighter. "I was beginning to think you'd never ask."

I slid into the pilot's seat, hands on the controls, adrenaline already kicking in.

The way I saw it, I had two options: run—which was obviously not happening—or fight, which, let's be honest, was way more my style.

I hit the comms and sent out a broadcast to our new friends.

"Hey there, fellas. I see you're tailing me. That's cute. But before you do something stupid, let me introduce you to my ship." I tapped the weapons system online, and Deadline hummed like a beast waking up from a nap. "She bites."

A pause.

Then, one of the ships fired up their weapons.

I grinned.

"Switch," I said, gripping the controls, "let's make this quick. I've got an article to finish."

And with that, we went to war.

Now, I'm not saying I'm the best pilot in the galaxy, but I am saying that three unmarked merc ships thinking they could outfly Deadline was adorable.

The second they powered up their weapons, I yanked us into a hard climb, letting their first volley sail harmlessly underneath us. Switch braced himself in the back seat, deadpan as ever.

"They're firing at us," he noted.

"You think?" I shot back, rolling us sideways to avoid another barrage. The ships split up, trying to flank us.

"Shall I return fire?" Switch asked.

I grinned. "Let's not be rude. Of course, you should return fire."

With a satisfying thunk, Deadline's cannons deployed. A moment later, the cockpit flashed red as Deadline let loose a volley of plasma rounds. One of the mercs' ships took a hit to the shields and veered off-course, spiraling to recover.

"First blood," I said cheerfully.

"The phrase is metaphorical," Switch reminded me.

"Not if they explode."

The second ship looped around, trying to get on my tail. Classic rookie mistake. I cut power for a split second, letting him overshoot, then punched it again, swinging Deadline back around so now I was on his tail.

I fired.

His shields held—for about two seconds. Then his engines coughed, sputtered, and died. His ship spun out, heading for a graceful crash landing on the nearest asteroid.

One down.

The third merc, apparently realizing he'd brought a knife to a gunfight, hit the afterburners and bolted.

"Oh, come on," I groaned. "Where's your sense of commitment?"

I reached for the weapons control again, but Switch stopped me. "Unnecessary. He has accepted his defeat."

"Yeah, but it'd be fun."

"Roxie."

I sighed and pulled my hand back. "Fine. Let the coward live."

The first ship, the one still limping from our opening volley, decided it wasn't quite dead yet and took one last desperate shot. The bolt of plasma clipped Deadline's rear shielding—just enough to make my consoles flicker.

"Oh, you jerk," I muttered. "That was brand new."

I whipped the ship around, locking onto the idiot with Deadline's heavy cannons.

Switch, ever patient, said, "You could let him retreat."

I narrowed my eyes at the enemy ship, then smiled.

"Yeah, okay." I hit the comms. "Hey, buddy? That was not your smartest move. But since I'm feeling generous, I'm going to give you a one-time offer."

I flipped a switch, charging up Deadline's biggest, meanest railgun. It glowed ominously on-screen.

"You leave. Right now. Or I turn you into space dust. Your call."

The merc didn't even hesitate. His ship spun around so fast he nearly lost control, then rocketed out of there like his engines were on fire.

I leaned back in my seat, satisfied.

Deadline powered down the weapons. "Conflict resolved."

"Was there ever any doubt?" I said, stretching. "Honestly, that was kind of a letdown."

"You are disappointed we were not in greater danger?"

"I'm just saying, if someone's gonna try to kill me, they should commit to it."

Switch shook his head. "I do not think that is how most people view combat."

"Most people are boring."

With a deep hum, Deadline settled back into cruising speed. The wreckage of one ship floated lifelessly in the distance, and the other two were long gone.

I grinned.

"Well," I said, "that was fun."

Switch didn't dignify that with a response.

Chapter 20: The Art of Selective Truth-Telling

I strutted into the newsroom like I owned the place—which, legally speaking, I absolutely did not. But confidence is everything, and I had enough confidence to fuel a small war.

Dobbs was waiting at her desk, arms crossed, eyes already exuding the kind of disappointment usually reserved for kids who flush their parents' credit chips down the drain.

"Vex."

"Chief."

She didn't say anything for a long moment, just stared at me, likely wondering if this was the day she finally strangled me with my own press credentials.

I dropped my datapad onto her desk. "One scandalous, shocking exposé, fresh off the presses. You're welcome."

She skimmed the first few lines, then sighed heavily and rubbed her temples. "I just got off a call with a very concerned insurance conglomerate that is definitely sending a hit squad after you."

"See? That's how you know it's good journalism."

Dobbs picked up the datapad, scrolled a bit, then looked back at me with something dangerously close to admiration. "I hate that I have to say this, but this might actually be your best piece yet."

I gasped. "Was that... a compliment?"

"Don't get used to it." She flicked the datapad back at me. "Now get out of my office before I change my mind and reassign you to celebrity gossip."

"Don't threaten me, Dobbs. You know I'd love that beat."

She waved me off, already turning to yell at some poor intern who'd apparently forgotten how deadlines worked.

Satisfied with another job well done (or at least done), I headed straight for *The Cosmic Catastrophe*, dragging Tucker Quinn along for the ride.

The bar—still so named because Tucker and I refused to learn its actual name—was the kind of place where the drinks were cheap, the floor was sticky, and the patrons were either dangerous criminals or just looked like them.

We slid into our usual booth. Tucker ordered something fruity. I ordered something strong.

"So," he said, grinning over the rim of his ridiculous pink drink, "how many times did you almost die this time?"

I leaned back, stretching dramatically. "Almost? Please. They tried to kill me, but obviously, I was too magnificent to be hit."

Tucker snorted. "So, let me get this straight. Three merc ships. Versus you, alone, in Deadline. And you didn't almost die?"

I waved a hand. "Oh, they thought they had me. They came in all sneaky, probably thinking they were gonna scare me into surrendering. But no. I was ready. I outmaneuvered them like a goddess of the skies."

He nodded. "Uh-huh. And Switch?"

I took a sip of my drink. "He was there."

Tucker smirked. "So what really happened?"

I glared at him. "How dare you."

"Roxie."

I sighed dramatically. "Fine. I may have been ever so slightly caught off-guard when the first shot grazed our shields."

Tucker's smirk grew. "And?"

"And Deadline may have made some very judgmental remarks about my flying while executing evasive maneuvers for me."

"And?"

"And Switch may have taken over weapons control because I was slightly busy yelling at Deadline about how I totally had it handled."

Tucker was outright laughing now. "So what you're saying is... your ship and your robot boyfriend saved your life again."

"He is not my robot boyfriend," I grumbled.

"Tell that to literally anyone who's ever seen you two bicker."

I ignored that. "Anyway, the important thing is I won."

"Thanks to your sentient ship."

"Which is mine, so technically, I still get credit."

Tucker lifted his glass in mock salute. "To Roxie Vex: greatest journalist, ace pilot, and the only woman I know who can start a war with three different corporations in a single week."

I clinked my glass against his. "And don't you forget it."

Chapter 21: The News We Truly Deserve

Tucker checked his wrist chrono, sighed, and downed the last of his ridiculous pink drink. "Well, I gotta go. Got an assignment."

That caught my attention. "Fluff piece?"

He nodded. "Oh yeah. Prime absurdity."

I tapped my fingers against my glass. "Huh."

Tucker raised an eyebrow. "Huh?"

"Huh as in... I think I wanna tag along."

His brows shot up. "You? The Roxie Vex, fearless investigative reporter, slayer of crime lords, and breaker of insurance policies, wants to do a fluff piece?"

I shrugged. "I dunno. I've never seen you work before. Kinda curious what the galaxy's greatest nonsense reporter does with his time."

Tucker grinned, clearly pleased. "Well, far be it from me to deny you the chance to witness true journalistic artistry. But we're taking my ship."

That made me hesitate. "Your ship?"

"Yep. Ol' Punchline."

I blinked. "You named your ship Punchline?"

He patted his chest proudly. "Of course. Because if it ever goes down, it's taking the joke with it."

That was... not reassuring.

I glanced at Switch, who had been standing silently nearby, likely already calculating the percentage chance of Tucker's ship immediately killing us upon takeoff. He said nothing, which meant the odds were probably not great.

I sighed. "Fine. But Deadline is following us."

Tucker rolled his eyes. "As if you'd ever go anywhere without your murder-pod."

I smiled sweetly. "I don't like to put my death in the hands of unreliable technology."

Tucker clapped me on the shoulder. "Then you are gonna love my ship."

Aboard the Punchline

The moment I stepped onto Tucker's ship, the lights flickered, a vent somewhere let out a very suspicious hissss, and something in the cockpit beeped like it had just remembered it was supposed to be on fire.

I froze. "Tucker."

"Yes, Roxie?"

"Why is your ship making death sounds?"

He waved a hand dismissively. "She's just saying hello."

A panel near the door promptly fell off and clattered to the floor.

Switch, who had taken one step inside and then stopped like he was reconsidering every life choice that had brought him here, tilted his head. "This vessel does not appear structurally sound."

"She's charming," Tucker corrected. "Deadline is all sleek, intimidating, and high-tech. Punchline has character."

I eyed the exposed wiring hanging out of a wall panel. "She also has electrical hazards."

Tucker flopped into the pilot's chair and started pressing buttons. Most of them lit up. "Relax. She hasn't killed me yet."

"Yet."

"Exactly." He flicked on the comms. "Deadline, you following?"

My ship's voice crackled through the speakers. "Affirmative. Scanning Punchline for potential catastrophic failures."

Tucker sighed. "Don't listen to her, baby," he cooed at his ship. "You're perfect just the way you are."

Something sparked near my feet. I took a careful step back. "Tucker, what is this assignment even about?"

"Oh, right." He grinned. "You ever heard of the Haunted Karaoke Machine of Zelo-5?"

Switch and I stared at him.

"No," I said flatly.

"Well, I have." He hit the thrusters, and the ship let out a deeply unsettling groan. "And we're gonna go meet it."

I buried my face in my hands. "I regret everything."

Chapter 22: The Haunted Karaoke Machine of Zelo-5

The flight to Zelo-5 was relatively uneventful—relative being the key word.

The Punchline only glitched twice. Once, when the artificial gravity flickered for about five seconds, leaving me floating in midair while Tucker casually sipped his drink like this was completely normal. The second time, when the ship's nav computer announced, in a very concerned tone, that we were currently inside a sun, which was news to all of us, including the very not-on-fire state of our ship.

"Just a software bug," Tucker said, smacking the console until the nav stopped screaming about impending doom.

Switch did not sit down for the entire flight.

Eventually, we landed in what I will generously describe as "mostly the right spot." The Punchline groaned in relief as the landing struts touched the ground. Something in the engine let out a clunk, but Tucker cheerfully ignored it and hopped out.

I followed, making a silent vow to hug Deadline when I got back.

The haunted karaoke machine was set up in the back of a grimy little dive bar run by an elderly Lizard-like guy named Grinko, who had exactly one eye, three teeth, and a cigarette that had been burning for so long I was pretty sure it was an artifact from another timeline.

Tucker pulled out his recorder and got right to work.

"So, Grinko," he said, leaning on the bar, "word on the street is, your karaoke machine is haunted."

Grinko took a long drag of his eternal cigarette. "Ain't haunted. Just cursed."

I blinked. "Oh, well, that's much better."

Tucker grinned and made a "go on" motion.

Grinko exhaled a slow cloud of smoke. "Machine's older than dirt, yeah? Was already here when I bought the place. Ain't normal, though. Picks the song for ya."

Tucker raised an eyebrow. "And?"

Grinko leaned in. "And it don't care who you are. Picks the song that tells your truth."

I snorted. "Oh no, not the terrifying power of lyrical self-reflection."

Tucker elbowed me. "Shhh. This is gold."

"People come from all over to test it," Grinko continued. "Some get love songs. Some get anthems. Some get ballads about regret."

Tucker tapped his recorder. "Any notable victims?"

Grinko chuckled darkly. "Yeah. Last month, a big-shot corporate exec from the megabank on Nexo-12 showed up, all puffed up. Got on stage, grabbed the mic, an' the machine picked I'm a Scoundrel and a Liar."

I nearly choked on my drink.

Tucker's eyes lit up. "No."

"Oh yeah." Grinko smirked. "Whole crowd laughed 'im outta the bar. He left so fast, he forgot his coat."

Tucker turned to me. "I love my job."

I wiped away tears of laughter. "I might love your job too."

Switch, standing stiffly nearby, did not look amused. "This assignment has no inherent value."

Grinko eyed him. "Wanna test it?"

Switch didn't even dignify that with a response.

After getting enough material to write what I could only assume would be Tucker's magnum opus, we headed back to the Punchline.

For the first time in forever, I had a blast just watching someone else work. Tucker was sharp, sarcastic, and knew exactly how to get the weirdest, funniest quotes out of people. I was still laughing when we strapped in for takeoff.

Switch, on the other hand, was done.

"We could have returned hours ago," he grumbled.

"Oh, lighten up, Switch." I kicked back in my seat. "Not every assignment has to be life-threatening."

"I prefer the life-threatening ones."

Tucker grinned. "See, that's why you two work. You run headfirst into death, and he's your designated buzzkill."

Switch sighed. "Your ship is malfunctioning again."

Tucker checked the console. "Nah, that's just the heater. It makes that noise when it's on."

"What noise?" I asked.

Just then, the ship let out an ungodly HHHHRRRRRNNNNGGGGHHHH that rattled my teeth.

Tucker flicked a switch. The sound stopped.

"See?" he said brightly. "Fixed."

I buried my face in my hands. "I can't believe I enjoyed this."

Tucker elbowed me. "Welcome to my world."

Deadline followed us the whole way back, but for once, she wasn't needed. Which, frankly, was probably the weirdest part of the entire trip.

Chapter 23: Crime, Champagne, and Cleavage

Dobbs tossed a datapad onto my desk with the usual amount of grace and affection. "New assignment."

I picked it up, skimmed the details, and grinned. "A smuggler? Ooo, Dobbs, you shouldn't have."

She leveled a look at me. "Don't get too excited. You're still working."

"Oh, of course," I said, already mentally picking out a dress. "Totally professional. No fun at all."

She sighed. "The party's on a yacht, the guy's a big deal, and you need to get him talking. I don't care how you do it, just get the story."

I leaned back in my chair. "Which means dressing up, drinking champagne, and rubbing elbows with the hoity-toity." I smiled. "This is my favorite kind of crime."

A few hours later, I was stepping onto a luxury yacht in a red evening gown that—if I turned too fast—might have legally counted as a felony.

Switch, as always, was my plus-one, dressed in his usual ensemble of massive and intimidating.

"You know," I said as I accepted a flute of champagne from a waiter, "I really should do more of these assignments."

Switch scanned the crowd. "Your interest in crime is unsettling."

I took a sip. "What can I say? I love a good scam. Especially when it comes with hors d'oeuvres."

The smuggler in question was a tall, silver-haired man named Marius Vale. He had the kind of easy confidence that said I could buy and sell you, but I won't, because I like the company.

I liked him immediately.

"Mister Vale," I purred as I slid onto the seat next to him. "Roxie Vex, Galactic Gazette."

He gave me a slow smile. "I know who you are."

That was either a good sign or a very bad one.

I twirled my glass. "Then you know I'm here for a story."

"I do." He motioned for the bartender to pour me another. "And you know I don't give interviews."

I clinked my glass against his. "Neither do crime lords, and yet, here we are."

Vale chuckled. "Touché."

The thing about smugglers is, they're a lot like reporters. They get information from all sorts of places, know things no one else does, and are excellent at dodging questions. Vale was no exception. He danced around my questions with expert precision, giving me just enough to be interesting, but not enough to be incriminating.

And honestly? That was fine.

Because the fun of this assignment wasn't just the story—it was the game.

By the time I made my exit, I had a half-decent article, a mild champagne buzz, and a new contact in my growing Rolodex of Questionable People.

Back aboard Deadline, I kicked off my heels and sighed happily. "That was fun."

Switch folded his arms. "You find illegal activity fun."

"Only when it involves yachts and expensive liquor." I stretched. "Besides, I got what I needed."

"For your article?"

"For future articles." I winked. "Marius Vale likes me. That means if something really juicy comes up, I might just get the tip-off before anyone else."

Switch sighed. "This is why Malloy drinks."

I grinned. "Speaking of which—let's get back to the Gazette. I feel like celebrating."

The bullpen at the Gazette was its usual chaotic mess, but when I strutted in—still in my dress, hair perfectly in place—the usual whistles and whoo-hoos followed.

I threw my arms out. "Please, please, hold your applause."

Tucker leaned on my desk. "So? How'd it go?"

I flopped into my chair. "Champagne. Crime. Expensive suits. Absolutely delightful."

Dobbs walked by, snatched my datapad, and muttered, "I swear to God, Vex, if this article reads like a dating profile—"

Tucker smirked. "So what now, oh great and glamorous journalist?"

I shrugged. "Now? I write the story." I tapped the side of my head. "And keep the real stories in here for later."

Tucker lifted his drink. "To later, then."

I clinked my water bottle against it. "To much later."

Switch, watching us, sighed. "This cycle of reckless behavior will never end."

I shot him finger guns. "Not if I can help it."

And with that, I got back to doing what I did best—writing the truth, dodging the consequences, and getting into just enough trouble to keep life interesting.

From the author,

Hello,

If you found this story as fun to read as I did to write, please leave a review to let others know your thoughts on it. I would greatly appreciate it.

Ben

Don't miss out!

Visit the website below and you can sign up to receive emails whenever Ben Patterson publishes a new book. There's no charge and no obligation.

https://books2read.com/r/B-A-HYYYC-KPFYF

BOOKS 2 READ

Connecting independent readers to independent writers.

Did you love *Fear and Journalism 2*? Then you should read *Fear and Journalism in the Andromeda Fringe*[1] by Ben Patterson!

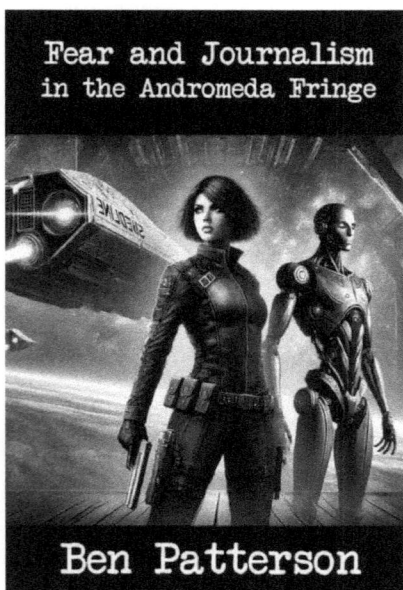

Roxie Vex isn't a cop—she's a reporter with a gun and a whole lot of attitude. Covering crime for the *Galactic Gazette*, she chases the galaxy's worst scumbags, dodging bullets, explosions, and bureaucratic nonsense along the way. When a deep-space colony reports unexplained disappearances, she follows the trail straight into the clutches of Baron Yorrik, a warlord running an illegal gladiator arena and a sinister slave trade. But Roxie's got more than just a sharp tongue and a fast trigger—she's got *Deadline*, her sentient spaceship, and *Switch*, her humanoid AI partner, both designed to keep her alive... whether she likes it or not.

Throw in a snarky fellow journalist, a grumpy ex-flame in the feds, and a wardrobe upgrade that's turning heads, and Roxie's latest assignment is more than just a job—it's personal. Lighthearted, fast-paced, and packed with action, *Roxie Vex: The Galactic Gazette Files* is a wild ride through crime, corruption, and cosmic chaos.

www.ingramcontent.com/pod-product-compliance
Ingram Content Group UK Ltd.
Pitfield, Milton Keynes, MK11 3LW, UK
UKHW040735250225
455493UK00015B/152